PATSY KELLY INVESTIGATES

No Through Road

There were three or four minutes of noise and scuffle until a loud scream stopped everyone. A young woman was found standing opposite a giant cement mixer. She was stock still as though stuck to the spot, her mouth wide open.

Eddie Wolf's face was visible, a ghastly bluish colour. It was as if he was peeking out of the mixer, except that he was still and stiff, not unlike the hardened cement that was holding him there. The fire brigade had had to cut him out of the cement mixer. Even then, his body was still half encased in concrete. He had to be taken, like that, in a van to the morgue where the pathologists had to chip off the remaining stuff.

A lifeless boy who would never move again.

It gave me a bad feeling.

POINT CRIME

PATSY KELLY INVESTIGATES

No Through Road

Anne Cassidy

■SCHOLASTIC

Scholastic Children's Books
Commonwealth House, 1–19 New Oxford Street,
London WC1A 1NU, UK
a division of Scholastic Ltd
London ~ New York ~ Toronto ~ Sydney ~ Auckland

First published by Scholastic Ltd, 1996

Copyright © Anne Cassidy, 1996

ISBN 0 590 13416 7

Typeset by TW Typesetting, Midsomer Norton, Avon

Printed by Cox & Wyman Ltd, Reading, Berks.

10 9 8 7 6 5 4 3 2 1

Contents

1
The Wolfboy

Eddie Wolf was murdered on Easter Monday. They found his body curled up in the drum of a cement mixer on the site of the new link road.

His lower half had been submerged in a residue of hard cement but above the waist, his chest and head had been visible, his face leaning against the rim of the mouth of the giant machine. His arms had been hanging lifelessly and on his neck and shirt was a dark brown stain that came from beneath his long matted hair. His eyes were closed but his mouth was open slightly as if he'd just been about to say something.

I only knew all this afterwards when I saw the police photos.

On the day itself Billy and I had been having a

drink in the front garden of a pub on the edge of Epping Forest. Even though it had been a bit chilly, we'd braved the fresh air alongside a cold looking family whose children were having races around the wooden tables. Billy had been talking about a new car he was going to buy.

"It's a Triumph Spitfire," he'd said, "a classic model. The engine's gone though and there's a good deal of rust on the chassis. I should be able to fix it up."

My mind hadn't really been on what Billy was saying. He often enthused about cars and I nodded my head or said "um" in the appropriate places. That's what we were like, an old married couple. We were used to each other.

It hadn't always been like that but on that particular Monday I wasn't really thinking about me and Billy. I was thinking about my mum's new boyfriend, Gerry, the mature student from her college. He had been around for a few weeks and had the irritating habit of calling me "Pats", as if I were plural.

My mum had started behaving oddly as well; singing first thing in the morning, endlessly flicking through women's magazines, trying the tester lipsticks in Boots and looking at herself in mirrors in department stores. She had also spent a small fortune on a new set of fitness clothes, leotards, sweats and joggers, flash trainers and sports shoes.

Gerry Lawrence wasn't the sporty type at all. He had tinted penny glasses and a hard round belly, suggesting several months of pregnancy. He had appeared at our front door a few weeks before.

"Is *she* in?" he'd said, leaning rakishly against the porch wall, the word "she" sounding suggestive, as if he were expecting Marilyn Monroe and not my mother to come down the hall stairs. Before I could answer, though, I heard her hurried footsteps and she sprang from behind me, smelling heavily of scent.

As she went out I'd said, "What time will you be in?" but she hadn't answered. The pair of them had giggled off up the path and I'd been left standing like an anxious parent.

"Look over there." Billy's voice had broken into my thoughts. I'd looked, expecting to find an example of some sort of vintage or rare car. Instead there was a group of people, coming along the road some hundred metres or so away, waving banners and chanting. Behind and alongside them were a couple of police cars and some PCs strolling along at the edge of the group. They came slowly along and the children from the next table were straining against the wooden fence of the pub garden to get out at them.

They were walking, marching even, towards the site of the new link road. I took a drink and tore open a bag of crisps. It was a colourful procession, mostly young people dressed in hippie-type clothes, lots of young kids running around as well as a few dogs looking bemused but along for the free walk.

The banners were home-made. One said, NO LINK ROAD, another said, PEOPLE BEFORE CARS. Some of them were singing quietly, a folk-song, not my favourite kind of music. Bit by bit people came out of the pub and stood in the garden watching them walk by, mumbling disapproval or laughing at them.

I began to feel annoyed. I was about to say something about it to Billy when he said, "Idiots! It makes me mad. The car is progress! They're acting as though it's like a nuclear weapon or something."

I bit my lip silently. Billy was nineteen, like me, but sometimes he sounded as though he were fifty.

"What about the pollution?" I said, in a low voice, not wishing to start a full scale debate in the pub garden. We'd been having arguments about the new road for weeks.

"Handled *sensibly*, the motor car is a modern miracle," Billy answered, looking after the demonstrators and shaking his head. I was instantly reminded of my uncle Tony, the man I work for, who often gave a sad shake of his head at the younger generation, women, or any kind of modern music.

I sat silently for a few minutes thinking of numerous things to say, arguments to make. I remembered something my mum's new boyfriend,

Gerry, had said a few days before: "Someone's got to put a stop to these monster roads, Pats. They're eating up the countryside."

I'd had a cartoon image in my head of a personified road, the end of it a big dark mouth that bit into the green fields and ate up anything in its way. It was a child's view but it had stuck with me. I wondered why he hadn't been on the demonstration. He'd been handing out leaflets against the new road down at the shopping centre the previous week.

"Want another drink?" Billy said, looking up from his car magazine, as though nothing unusual had happened, as though we'd been discussing the weather or the price of fish.

"Nope," I'd said pointedly. "I want to go home."

It was about six o'clock that evening that the news of the dead boy came through. My mum and I were in the kitchen toasting some bread when Gerry Lawrence arrived. My mum bounced down the hall to open the door for him. I could hear them murmuring as they came back into the room. Gerry looked different than usual, his face grim, his mouth in a straight line. He took his glasses off.

"Something terrible's happened, Patsy," my mum said. "One of the boys from Gerry's group has been killed on the link road site."

Gerry plonked down on to the chair. He seemed

to have doubled in weight and, without his glasses, his eyes had sunk back into his head.

"What happened?" I said, pulling a chair out to sit down on.

Gerry shook his head from side to side. He honestly looked as though he was on the brink of tears.

"One of the boys from the Fresh Air Campaign, Eddie Wolf. He was only seventeen and he's dead," my mum said, putting her fingers into Gerry's hair and stroking it.

"I know his dad," Gerry said with emotion in his voice. "And his mum."

The details came out on the local news the next day. Most of them I'd already got, in bits and pieces, from Gerry. Billy had even rung me up mid-evening and told me a couple of things he'd heard down at his local pub.

Eddie Wolf had been one of the protesters, he'd been involved in some of the demonstrations in the previous weeks. He'd been one of the kids who had chained himself to one of the big trees on the common that was being knocked down to make way for the road. He was meant to take part in the demonstration on Easter Monday, the one that Billy and me saw from the pub garden, but he hadn't turned up.

After they had left us, the protesters had walked slowly up by the wooden fences that cordoned the whole area off. There'd been a plan hatched before, apparently, that on a certain signal they'd all stop singing and make a run for the main gate, flinging it open and run into the site, jumping on the equipment, chaining or tying themselves to it.

It took the police and the security men by surprise. The gates fell back against the crowd and once they were in they all ran towards the machinery.

There were three or four minutes of noise and scuffle until a loud scream stopped everyone. A young woman was found standing opposite a giant cement mixer. She was stock still as though stuck to the spot, her mouth wide open.

Eddie Wolf's face was visible, a ghastly bluish colour. It was as if he was peeking out of the mixer, except that he was still and stiff, not unlike the hardened cement that was holding him there. The fire brigade had had to cut him out of the cement mixer. Even then, his body was still half encased in concrete. He had to be taken, like that, in a van to the morgue where the pathologists had to chip off the remaining stuff.

I could just imagine them; men in white coats, tiny hammers and chisels in their hands, their foreheads creased in concentration. They must have looked like artists, sculpting the form of a boy.

A lifeless boy who would never move again.

It gave me a bad feeling.

2
The Office Clerk

My uncle Tony was already in his office when I got there on Wednesday morning. The glass door that said ANTHONY HAMER INVESTIGATIONS INC. was ajar. The lights were on and the kettle had just been boiled. He had taken two of the china cups and saucers that we kept for visitors and opened a new packet of biscuits.

He had actually made the tea himself. I thought that it must have been someone important he was with. I looked through the mottled glass of his door but I couldn't see who it was. Then I noticed a woman's navy blue mac on the coat stand. I wondered if he had a new client.

A few minutes later he called me on the intercom.

"Patricia, come in, will you, and bring the insurance files."

When I went in Heather Warren was sitting on the soft chair, her shoes off and her feet up under her as if it were evening and she was relaxing, watching the TV. On the palm of one hand was her saucer and in the other was her cup. On the arm of the chair was a small plate of pink wafery biscuits.

"Hello, Patsy," she said, a biscuit half in her mouth.

I smiled and put the files down, then went back to my own desk.

Heather Warren was a detective inspector in the local CID. She and I had known each other since I'd got involved in a couple of murder cases that the police had been investigating. She liked me, although there were times during the investigations that she'd acted as though I were a real pain in her backside. When the cases were over and the murderers behind bars she was full of praise for me and spent ages trying to persuade me to join the police or go to university; anything rather than be an *underachieving clerk for your uncle Tony*.

I liked her as well. She was prickly but honest; she was hard and bossy but determined and caring.

My uncle Tony, the private investigator, didn't like her but pretended he did. He'd been a policeman once himself but had left a number of years ago. My aunt Geraldine hadn't liked him spending such a lot of time away from the family. Occasionally he needed the help of the police and so, against his better judgement, he'd attempted to make friends with Heather. That was probably why she was in the office with him, swapping information about wrongdoings.

Heather hadn't been taken in by my uncle's box of chocolates or his cheery phone calls. I'd recently asked her why she bothered with him. He was vain, overweight, over-opinionated and dreadfully sexist. She'd just clicked her tongue and drunk her glass of wine down in one go. "Look Patsy, in this business, you never know who might be useful one day. You just never know."

I began to sort through the work I had to do for that day. There were some letters to type and some bills to pay. I had a few phone calls to make and some documents to deliver. I also had some photos to pick up from the developers. All of it easy stuff that a kid on work experience could have done.

It didn't have to be like that. After my success in the two previous cases my uncle had offered to let me work alongside him. Important jobs, surveillance, meeting clients, making enquiries. He said he'd actually been impressed with my work although I had the feeling that he wanted me where he could keep an eye on me. Even so, it meant I could have had real experience of investigating crime.

Billy had been pleased when I'd told him.

"Well, that's what you wanted, wasn't it? To be taken seriously? To be treated like an equal?"

It had been. Once.

After the last case I'd been involved in had closed I'd been exhilarated for a while. All sorts of *I told you so*'s had been on the tip of my tongue. People kept congratulating me. It seemed, for a short while, as though everyone had heard about it and my part in the discovery of the murderer. I'd been in a euphoric mood. I'd worn my most flamboyant hats and treated myself to several new bits of clothing. I'd even got a bit more than romantic with Billy on a few occasions.

Then, after a few weeks had passed I got a kind of delayed reaction. I kept remembering the dead girl's face, seeing kids around who resembled her. I'd even dreamt about her a couple of times. I'd go out to buy something and find myself, inexplicably, walking around the area that she had lived in. I even went to her grave a couple of times.

I'd realized, slowly, that it hadn't just been a case. It had been the end of someone's life.

Depression had soaked through me like a slow drizzle. It left me feeling weak and uncomfortable; cold and miserable. Antony Hamer Investigations Inc. was the last place I wanted to be and picking up the sharp, broken pieces of some stomach-turning crime was the last thing I wanted to do.

I'd taken some time off and spent it with my dad. He lives in Birmingham and I stayed in his flat. We'd gone to some plays and films and spent a lot of time walking round museums. It had been like a different life. We'd also sorted out prospectuses for universities and I'd decided that going back to education was the right thing to do. When I came back and told my mum and Tony there was almost a family celebration, great sighs of relief. It was as if I'd been toying with a career in the Mafia and had finally decided to reject it. My uncle Tony had toasted me with a glass of fizzy white wine and said, "A good decision, Patsy. You've had some luck but you need to leave crime enforcement to those who can handle it!"

I'd kept my mouth shut, not wanting to get into an argument with him. I still needed the clerical job. The salary was OK and the work was easy. I had five months to get through and then I'd pack away my office skirts and blouses and get back to doing what I should have done last year, being a student.

It had taken people by surprise, my change of heart, especially Billy. When I'd come back from being with my dad he'd said, "There's something different about you, Pat. I can't put my finger on it."

And he was right. I'd decided what I wanted to do and it wasn't anything to do with crime investigation.

I sorted through the pile of bills I had to pay. British Telecom, British Gas, a couple for electronic equipment and an expenses bill from Bob Franks, a man who sometimes did freelance work for my uncle. I got the payment documents out and the cash book and began to write out the cheques. The office door opened and I could hear Heather coming out.

"OK Tony, I'll see what I can do. Don't forget about that other business though."

"I won't." I could hear my uncle's voice.

Heather picked up her coat from the stand and then came and sat on the corner of my desk. She got a small mirror out of her bag and looked into it.

"Haven't seen you for ages, Patsy. What about lunch?"

"That would be nice," I said, genuinely. I was surprised at her being so concerned with the way she looked. Then I noticed that she had a very smart suit on and her hair had been styled. She'd lost weight as well. She replaced the mirror.

"Come down to the station, about one. I should be able to get away."

When she left I was struck by the left-over scent that was in the air. I looked down at my brown A-line skirt and loose cream blouse. I tried to think back to the morning and remember whether I'd put make-up on or not. I couldn't even remember combing my hair.

I shrugged my shoulders to no one in particular.

A while later I took the cheques in for my uncle to

sign. He was running a clothes brush over his jacket, humming a tune. When he finished he went and stood in front of a wall mirror and, using his fingers, combed his hair away from his ears.

"Tony, can you sign these and I'll get them off in the post," I said, one hand on my hip.

"Sure, sure," Tony said as though he was doing me a great big favour.

He walked back to his desk and sat heavily down on his swivel chair. The light from the window showed up his greying sideburns. It wouldn't be long before my aunt Geraldine got rid of those signs of ageing. Then my uncle would arrive at work with a shining mop of jet black hair that looked as though it had been coloured with shoe polish.

"Tell me something, Patricia."

"Yes?" I said.

My uncle has always insisted on calling me Patricia even though everyone in my family, my mum, Dad, cousins, my aunt Geraldine, called me some shorter version of it. In the midst of the Patsys and Pat or even Tricia, my uncle maintained my full name. It was like some unconscious crusade against slipping standards. It also meant that he always sounded formal with me and there was inevitably some distance between us.

"What do you make of this chap, Gerry, that your mother's going out with?"

"He's OK," I said, surprised that Tony would

bring the subject up in the office. He didn't usually talk about the family or personal matters.

"Only I didn't take to him much, when she brought him round the other week."

"Oh, why not?" I said.

I didn't really need an answer. Even though Tony and Gerry were about the same age and build, they were poles apart. Tony, always immaculately dressed, was a family man. He owned his own house and had two cars. His daughter and son were both in good careers and his wife a model home-maker. Gerry, on the other hand, was a twice divorced father of two grown-up kids who shared a flat with some kids half his age. He was always talking about politics and usually, on Saturdays, he was outside the Exchange giving out some leaflets about the new road.

"He's, he's not what you'd call *stable*," he said, searching for the word.

"He's funny though," I said, unsure as to why I was sticking up for him. He wasn't my favourite person.

"Yes, that may be, that may be. But it doesn't pay the rent," Tony said mysteriously.

I couldn't argue with that so I went back into my office.

At lunchtime, on my way to meet Heather, I picked up a local paper. The front page was all about the death of the boy on the link road site. The headline read, WOLFBOY FOUND DEAD IN CEMENT MIXER; underneath, in dark print it said, *Edward Wolf, seventeen-year-old unemployed roads activist from Epping was found dead inside a cement mixer on Easter Monday. Police sources say that foul play is not suspected.*

I raised my eyebrows.

At least it wasn't murder.

3
Lunch

We had lunch in a pasta restaurant in the Exchange shopping centre. For three quid you could eat as much as you wanted. Heather had a small plate of pasta and a glass of fizzy water. I was on to my second plate of spaghetti in cream sauce. I also had a large Coke and some garlic bread.

I was eating because I felt awkward, nervous. I liked Heather but sometimes conversation was difficult. In some ways I hardly knew her at all. That was why, after we'd talked about my going to university, I brought up the only other subject that we had in common.

"I heard about that boy on the road site, Eddie Wolf."

"Awful business that," Heather said.

"But no need for an investigation, you think. Not murder."

Heather shook her head, while putting a single tube of pasta in her mouth. She was either on a strict diet or just not very hungry. I noticed again her careful make-up and wondered what had brought about the concern with her appearance. Eventually she said, "No, I was with the father when he made the identification. Poor man. He had to be physically held up by two officers. I thought, for a moment, he was going to faint."

"Was it a mess then, the body?" I said, not really wanting to hear.

"No. It had been cleaned up but, you know, seeing your loved ones like that, it's almost unthinkable."

I took a forkful of food and began to pass it from side to side in my mouth. I said, "In the newspaper, it said that there was no foul play suspected. What do you think happened?"

"Well, it's for the coroner to determine the exact circumstances of the death. Oh my God, I'm sounding like a policewoman again," she laughed and seemed to be sharing a joke with herself. "Look, the people in this protest group were pretty badly shaken up by it all. They've been really helpful though and told us everything they know. It seems as though this kid, Eddie, along with a friend, what was his name? George somebody, decided to try and tamper with some of the equipment, you know, take

18

bits from the engines, generally hold up the building work. It's been done on other sites. That's why the security is meant to be so tight."

"How did they get in?"

"We're just not sure. No sooner do the security men mend a hole in the fencing than another one appears somewhere else. They arranged a diversion, some protesters up at the far end of the site, chanting and singing songs. Naturally, all the security headed in that direction. They got in and headed for the most expensive equipment. No one heard them. The demonstration at the other end lasted for about half an hour, long enough to disable the vehicles and clear off out."

"Sounds like a military operation," I said, imagining them in fatigues with their faces blacked out.

"Commando stuff. You wouldn't see women acting like that."

I didn't remind Heather of the women who had been chained to the trees.

"The point is that Eddie Wolf's injuries don't suggest there was any foul play. He had a number of knocks on his skull and dozens of bruises and abrasions on his body surface. What we think was that he was in the process of loosening bolts, cutting wires, whatever, and somehow the mixer was turned on by mistake by the other boy. Eddie, caught unawares, was thrown about inside the drum, awful, like a cat in a tumble drier. He must have hit his head quite badly on the inside of the mixer. The actual wound areas suggest a series of flat blows, you know, different from, say, a blow with a hammer. The other boy, George somebody, must have taken one look at what had happened and run off."

"What did he actually die of?"

"Well, the blows to the head were bad enough. There's a possibility that he might have survived if he had got medical care. But what with all the other injuries and the temperature, it was below freezing you know, at this time of year!"

"Was he conscious, do you think?" I forked up the rest of my pasta and thought of the injured boy lying in the mixer all night.

"No, I don't think so."

"And the other boy, George? What does he say?"

"He's not around, scarpered. The people we've spoken to say that he's not likely to surface again. You know the type, homeless, no family. All we've got is a name. The people from the protest group won't give any information on where he might be."

"Isn't that a bit suspicious?"

"I don't think so, Patsy. I think the whole thing was an Action Man type adventure that went wrong."

I gave a half smile. Heather wasn't fond of Male Ways. I finished my Coke and looked at my watch.

"I'll have to go," I said.

"OK, I'll get the bill, my treat. You can pay next time!"

I nodded my head but wondered whether there would be a next time. Heather and I lived in different worlds. As we were leaving I commented on the way she looked.

"You look really good, Heather. Have you lost weight?"

"Just a bit," she said, her face beaming with pleasure. I felt my own lunch sitting heavily round the waistband of my skirt. Maybe I should just have had one plate of pasta.

"Truth is, Patsy, I felt myself slipping into middle age. I've made a new resolution. To get out more, meet new people, look after my health. Not men or romance. I'm not looking for a husband or anything like that." She laughed. "I just want to have a healthier lifestyle. That's what the diet is all about."

I didn't ask her what the make-up and the nice suit were about. I said goodbye, pulled my own stomach in and walked on through the shopping centre. If Heather wanted to find a boyfriend, at her age, it was up to her. My mum had managed it after all.

I walked back to the office wondering what I was going to do with myself. Not that afternoon, I knew what I was doing then; going back to the office to make some phone calls for my uncle Tony, the detective.

I was thinking of the next five months before I went to university. My life seemed to be on hold until then. I felt like a video that had been paused, a story that had stopped in the middle.

Because nothing was happening to me I'd taken to living in the future. I'd found myself making elaborate plans for university, getting lost in daydreams of how it would be: moving into halls, trying to live on a grant, finding a house or flat to share with other students. I was even looking forward to the studying bit, seeking out the library, booking out a computer to use, sifting through books to pluck out bits of information. Taking great wads of rough notes and hewing them into a piece of writing that explained something to someone.

I'd given up living in the present. My excitement at being a detective had dissipated and now it seemed as though I was stuck in a long traffic jam with nowhere to go and no way to get out of it.

I looked around at the street I was in. There were cars and lorries in a long queue on both sides, fumes coming out of their rear ends, some blatantly huffing small clouds of brown gas into the air. The noise seemed heavy as though it were weighing on my shoulders. A horn sounded and I found myself jumping.

I held my breath and crossed the road towards the office.

4
Murder

It was a Monday morning three weeks later when my uncle called me into his office to talk about Eddie Wolf.

I'd been late for work because an accident had blocked the High Street. I'd got in about nine-fifteen, clicked the kettle on and sat crossly down at my desk. I wondered who it was my uncle had in his office, then after a while, I lapsed into thinking about Billy.

It had been nearly two weeks since I'd seen him. That was almost a record. At no time in the past six or seven years had I been out of touch with Billy for so long. When we were at school we'd been in the same groups for various subjects and the same form. Even so, I'd often popped round to his house on odd evenings just to see what he was doing.

After his parents got killed I made a point of seeing him daily, ringing him late at night to see what sort of day he'd had, including him in my own family arrangements. When he'd dropped out of school I used to walk home the long way, round by his house, buy a couple of doughnuts and spend some time there. Since I left school myself we'd seen quite a lot of each other during the day. He tested the cars he was rebuilding while teaching me to drive at the same time. From time to time our friendship had gone further. There'd been a number of kisses, some urgent hugging and hand holding.

It never developed though. The next time we saw each other we would always back off, refrain from mentioning the passionate episodes, stand rigidly apart, avoiding looking each other in the eye. We were like kids in a game of dares, dipping our toes into dangerous waters and running back, far away.

And lately, instead of being warm and friendly, things had become strained. We'd had some down-right rows, especially over the issue of the new road and the demonstrations. When Eddie Wolf had been killed Billy had shrugged his shoulders. I'd been so angry with him I'd hardly been able to speak.

We made friends though but since then things had been awkward. I was supposed to go to the cinema with him a couple of weeks before but he'd cried off at the last minute with a cold. Since then

I'd rung a few times but there'd been no answer. He'd rung the office once and left a message on the answer-phone and I'd tried to get back to him without success. After that I'd left it.

He could ring me if he wanted. It had been almost two weeks since we'd spoken.

My uncle's office door opened and broke my train of thought.

"Ah, Patricia. I need you," he said.

I picked up my note pad and made towards him. I was quite relieved to be able to stop thinking about Billy. Our friendship was in a quagmire and I didn't know what to do about it.

Inside Tony's office there was a man and a woman seated in the soft chairs.

"Patricia," Tony said. "I want you to meet Mr and Mrs Wolf. They want you to help them find the person who murdered their son, Eddie."

My uncle handed me a cup of tea and was giving me several encouraging smiles and referring to things I'd done in the past, the two murder cases that I'd been involved in. I was puzzled. I'd told Tony quite clearly that I didn't want to be involved in the investigative side of the business. I thought it was what he'd wanted. He'd seemed delighted at the time.

Mr and Mrs Wolf were looking at my uncle with admiration in their eyes. They'd been taken in by the office, the oak desk, the swivel chair, the words "Private Investigator" in gold on the window. They were clinging on to their cups and saucers, listening to his every word.

They were both pale and looked as though they'd dressed up for the appointment. The man was wearing a three-piece suit and shirt and tie. He kept moving his shoulders about and touching the knot of the tie as though he were uncomfortable in it. He was big, taking up much of the sofa space. He looked about my dad's age but his face was rugged, windblown.

The woman sat very close to him, her side disappearing into his. She was thin with strawberry blonde hair, the type that looked a bit like candy floss. She had a fitted suit on, dark grey, and a black handbag and shoes to match. She was very still for most of the time, her head only moving a fraction as my uncle moved around the room. From time to time she took a sip of tea and looked cautiously over at me.

When my uncle stopped speaking he looked expectantly in my direction. Not having listened, I just responded with a smile. Was he expecting me, after all I'd said, to get involved in another *murder*?

"You see," Mr Wolf spoke, "when our son was found dead…"

He paused for a moment as though trying to control himself. I noticed that his wife seemed to move even closer to him, visibly to shrink a little, only her stiff pink hair seemed boldly unmoved.

"We thought, well the police thought, it was an accident. Yes," he took a breath, "they thought it was an accident. And of course, even to us, it looked that way. It didn't seem to us anything more than one of those terrible things. You know, like two boys playing by a river, one of them falling in and drowning and the other running away."

He smiled briefly, but his wife had put the palm of her hand across her mouth. There was silence for a minute while I found myself biting my lip.

"It was hard to bear," Mr Wolf gave a light laugh, "our only son. Not what you'd call the brightest of boys, oh no. But then we aren't what you'd call educated people. No, no. I'm a steel erector myself and Lizzie here works for the council." He replaced his cup and saucer and took his wife's hand in his. "He'd even been in some trouble, thieving, getting into fights."

"But not for a long time. He'd put all that behind him." Mrs Wolf spoke, a heavy, throaty voice, quite out of keeping with her tiny, thin frame.

"Yes, yes. He'd been in a scheme run by some voluntary workers. You know, building, painting, decorating, stuff like that. We thought he might get a job out of it.

"And the 'Fresh Air Campaign'."

"Yes, yes," Mr Wolf seemed momentarily

annoyed, "he got involved with all these campaigners. No roads, no cars. I don't know what. At the time, we didn't think there was any harm in it. It seemed better to us than him hanging round street corners, getting into trouble with the law."

"It gave him something to think about," Mrs Wolf said.

"Anyway," Mr Wolf seemed to pull himself together, "the reason we are here is because a couple of days ago the boy who was with Eddie, George Exon, he rang us."

"The one who disappeared?" I asked, interested, in spite of the heaviness inside my chest.

"Yes. Ran off. The police say he was probably scared but..." Mr Wolf shrugged.

"We were out," Mrs Wolf said, "and he left a message on the answer-phone."

"I have it, you see, for business."

"We have the tape here. We've already shown it to the police."

"That's where we got your name, from Inspector Warren."

Mr Wolf held the tape up and my uncle took it and placed it into a cassette player. He pressed the ON button and the four of us sat quietly and listened. Mr Wolf's voice sounded for a few seconds and then a much higher voice spoke, hurriedly and breathlessly.

"This is Georgie Exon. I ... I don't know how to say

this but the stuff the cops are saying about Eddie is wrong. It weren't an accident like everyone thought... I was there. I thought Eddie and me were going in to break up the machinery but when we gets in there he goes, come on, there's something I want to look at. Then he goes into the house. I tells him to get out, so that we can do what we came to do but he goes I'll only be a minute, there's something I want to find. I stand there not knowing what to do and then I think I see someone coming across the site. I panic and run away. Eddie was on his own then, see, in that house. Somebody put him in the machine. It weren't an accident..."

Mr and Mrs Wolf hardly moved at all while the tape was playing. I could see the woman imperceptibly mouthing the words, as though she'd listened to it over and over again. I looked at her hand dwarfed by her husband's. Her pink hair suddenly looked washed out, see-through, fragile, just like the rest of her.

"The police don't seem to think it holds much weight. They've searched the derelict houses. They say that there was no sign that anyone else had been there. They say that there was no *reason*, no *motive*, for anyone to kill Eddie."

"They won't ignore it, they've said that," Mr Wolf said, gruffly, nodding his head.

"But, with the verdict being accidental death, they'll just keep it on their books. If anything comes to light..."

"Anything else turns up…"

"Then they'll follow it."

"Did you speak to Heather?" I said.

"I did. And she gave me your name. She said that if I wanted to pay someone to look into the case then you were a good person to ask. She gave me your uncle's phone number."

"I see," I said. Both of them were looking at me directly. Inside my head there was an argument going on. *Keep away from it, let someone else deal with it*. Mrs Wolf leant over and picked her handbag up and pulled something out of it. It was a photograph in a small frame. I took it.

A young man on a bike. His hair was long, parted in the middle, hanging down by the side of his face. He was smiling and had his thumb up. He had some kind of T-shirt on that said FRESH AIR FOR LIFE.

"That was taken the day before he died," Mrs Wolf said, her deep voice breaking.

"OK," I said, standing up. "I can't promise anything but we should be able to look into it."

There it was. I'd said *yes*, I couldn't back out after that.

5
The End of a Friendship

After Mr and Mrs Wolf had gone I sat down at my desk and flicked through the notes I'd made. There were also lists of friends and relevant addresses that the Wolfs had brought with them. I put the stuff into an envelope folder and sat looking for a moment at the photo of Eddie Wolf taken the day before he died.

He was looking directly at the camera and his smile was mischievous. I almost felt like smiling back.

There he was alive, full of beans, his T-shirt bearing the ironic line, FRESH AIR FOR LIFE. Then the next day he was a statue, something you might find in a modern art gallery.

My uncle had gone to lunch after thanking me for

agreeing to work on the case. He'd said it stiffly though, begrudgingly. He was miffed that the Wolfs had specifically asked for me. He still thought of himself as the boss though, he'd made that clear. He was going to deal with the "adult" side of the case, the building site, the road contractors, the police. It was up to me to talk to the young people, the pro-testers, Eddie Wolf's friends.

I dialled Billy's number and he answered almost immediately.

"Hi, Billy, it's Patsy. I wondered if you fancied meeting for lunch?"

He sounded pleased to hear from me and we arranged to meet in a café down near where he lived. It was a greasy spoon and instantly I had a craving for sausage and chips.

Billy was already there when I arrived. He was reading a newspaper and smiled when I sat down. We ordered some food and then there was an awkward silence. Eventually I said, "What you been doing?" I had my hands loosely clasped together.

"This and that," he said, looking shyly at me. "I've been working on a new car..." He seemed to stop mid-sentence, unsure as to whether to continue.

"Yes, what sort?" I said, trying to be friendly, to bury the arguments that we'd had about the new road.

"It's a VW," he said. "1600, GT."

"Great," I said, none the wiser, "are you respraying?"

We went on like that for a while. Short wooden questions that neither of us really wanted to bother with. We stopped when the woman who ran the café brought over our food.

"It's nice to see you," Billy said suddenly, as I was in the middle of putting a chip into my mouth.

"Yeah," I said, genuinely pleased. He looked well, his hair a bit longer, his shirt was new, one that I'd not seen before.

We ate without speaking for a while, the way we had done for years, not really worrying about the silences. When I'd almost finished I said, "Oh, guess what! I've got a case of my own. At least, something I'm in charge of."

"What is it?" he said, pushing his empty plate away.

"You remember that boy who was killed on the new link road building site, on Easter Monday? Eddie Wolf? Well, his parents think it might be murder…"

I was about to go and tell him the details but I was stopped in my tracks. He rolled his eyes as soon as I'd mentioned the new link road.

"What's the matter?" I said, gripping my knife and fork more aggressively than I needed to.

"Road protesters!" He shook his head from side to side.

"The boy was *killed*, though," I said, trying hard to keep my voice down. He went on, though, as if I hadn't spoken.

"Three times in the past few weeks I've been stuck in jams while they parade around the streets, blocking the traffic. And next Saturday there's to be a massive demonstration and all the roads round here will be closed. Defend the Air, they've called it."

I knew about the demonstration. My mum was going on it. She'd asked me to go as well.

"They break the law," he continued, "and then terrible things happen. Look, I'm not saying it isn't sad that the kid died but he shouldn't have been there."

"He might have been MURDERED," I said.

Billy picked up his newspaper and shook it with annoyance. I stood up, leaving some of my meal. I got a couple of pound coins out of my pocket and threw them on the table.

He looked up when the coins spun and settled.

"What's the matter?" he said. He had a puzzled expression on his face.

I'd always known that there was something of the old man about Billy. When his parents had been killed he'd had to grow up very quickly. Even before that, though, he was the sensible, sober type. The model citizen. He knew his rights but he also knew his place.

I sat down again.

"We're on different planets, Billy," I said. "You're just blinded by the fact that you love cars. They're like gods to you. You can't see anything else. These people have got a fair argument. They have a point of view. Surely they're entitled to have their say?"

"I'm not saying they haven't got a right to their point of view but..." He sighed and started to fold his newspaper up before putting it down beside his plate. "I'd better get back..."

"What's so wrong with free speech?" I said.

He stood up, pulled a fiver out of his pocket and pushed my two pound coins back at me. "There's nothing wrong with free speech, Pat. Put your money away. Lunch was my treat."

I watched his back go out the door and disappear up the road.

I got up, put the fiver on the counter and walked out of the café.

On the way back to the office I walked round by the new link site. I was downhearted. I wondered what on earth I was going to do about Billy. I stopped and looked at a series of posters that had been put up about the demonstration the following Saturday: *DEFEND THE AIR! Meet at the town hall and march the length of the link road. Stop the killer roads.* I almost laughed. It was like a poster for a bad movie: *Stop the killer tomatoes!* I wished Billy was there so that we could both laugh at it.

The new roadworks ran from an intersection roundabout on the M11, to the High Road, about three miles. The whole area was surrounded by wire netting or, in some places, a wooden fence. The problem area was close to the High Road and stretched for about half a mile along beside the tracks of the Central line tube. I walked alongside it and looked through the wire netting. It had been an area of large Victorian houses, detached, most of them, surrounded by cultivated gardens, giant shrubs and hearty trees. Many of the houses had been demolished and where they had once stood there was a small mountain of rubble, ornate iron trellis and shattered leaded windows in among the crumbling bricks and broken roof tiles. All the greenery had gone. There were only stumps of trees left doggedly sticking out of the ground.

Further on I went up to one of the viewing panels in a newly erected fence. There were about four old houses left standing amid the giant mechanical diggers and trucks. Alongside, near a track, were a couple of expensive cars parked at angles, a BMW and a Mercedes. A couple of workmen in donkey jackets were standing around talking, one of them looking at papers, the other pointing to parts of the site. A man in a light grey double breasted suit was in the middle, adjusting his safety helmet, taking it on and off as if it just wouldn't fit him. He looked funny, out of place, probably some council bureaucrat dipping his nose into the dirty work. He seemed interested in the old houses, sitting amid the rubble, like survivors of a bombing raid. I wondered if it were those houses that George Exon had been talking about. Had Eddie Wolf been looking in there for something when someone had stumbled on him? It seemed a vague, unlikely story. I walked on.

The whole area was guarded by security men. As I went past they stood in twos or threes, some talking into two-way radios, some looking closely at me, their eyes following me as I went in and out of their field of vision.

Gerry Lawrence, my mum's boyfriend, had told us that there'd been a lot of trouble on the site after Eddie Wolf had been found dead. The security firm that had had the contract had been sacked and a new company brought in. They had emerald green uniforms on, with the words SAFECO in gold across the back. On their heads they had yellow helmets. They looked like a bizarre private army. Gerry said some of them had other jobs, as bouncers in clubs. He said they were as far from being boy scouts as you could get.

I wandered slowly past, wondering exactly where Eddie and George had got in. That was my uncle's first job, to go to the site the next day and talk again to the people involved. It would mean a trip to the old security firm and a visit to the offices of the company who had the contract for building the road.

Me, I had said I would pick up some paperwork from Heather Warren and then go and find Eddie Wolf's friends. I looked at my watch. It was still early. I decided to make a start.

Back at the office I cleaned my glasses, laid out Heather's paperwork on the desk and started to read through it. She had photocopied several statements taken at the building site which I put aside for my uncle. She'd also given me a summary of background details about Eddie Wolf, some of which I had from his parents.

Eddie Wolf was an only child. His dad was Leslie Wolf, forty-seven, steel erector. Heather had spoken to him and scribbled the words, *intelligent man, total incomprehension at what's happened*. His mum was Elizabeth Wolf, forty-two, care assistant, local council old people's home. Heather had written, *reserved, leans on the husband a lot*.

They'd lived on the Ivy Gardens Estate for the last ten years or so.

Eddie had gone to the local comprehensive, Riverside. An officer had been to the school and talked to the teachers there. Eddie had been a problem for a number of years, truanting, getting involved with a local gang of boys. That was where he'd picked up the nickname, *Wolfboy*. Eventually he'd got into trouble with the police. He'd been charged along with another boy for some vandalism, as well as trying to use a stolen cheque card that he'd said he'd found.

Through his probation officer he'd got involved in the Second Chance Project. It was based in a building that used to be a primary school and was staffed by some paid workers but mostly by volunteers. That was how my mum's boyfriend, Gerry, had got to know Eddie.

In the envelope from Heather there was a photo-copy of a map of the road site. It was hand-drawn, rough, and with the names of roads scribbled here and there. Towards one end was an X. This was where Eddie's body had been found. It looked like a treasure map.

There was also a small plastic wallet with the words, *scene of crime* written on it. These were the photos taken of Eddie Wolf's body. I tipped them out on to the table and looked at them.

I'd seen photos of dead bodies before. I'd even discovered an actual body once. It was still grim though. Two or three of the pictures were of Eddie while he was still in the drum of the cement mixer. His eyes were closed but his mouth was slightly open, his head resting to the side. His arms were just hanging lethargically. His shoulders looked rounded and he was hunched over. If the mixer had turned thirty centimetres or so more he would have been lying on his back.

The other photos were of the body on the morgue

table. I flinched when I looked. The cement had been chipped off but he lay on his side, his knees up in a kind of foetal position. They hadn't been able to straighten him out. Rigor mortis had left him bent up for eternity.

I picked out the photo his mother had given me. He'd had that heavy straight hair, the kind I would have loved. It was parted in the middle and shone as if it had just been washed. I looked at the morgue photo. His hair was matted and dusty. I turned both photos over, not wanting to look any more.

I got my note pad out and wrote down a list of things I wanted to do and people I needed to see. I noticed that the Second Chance Project was open until ten every evening and thought that I might as well start there.

It was getting late and I knew my uncle wasn't coming back so I turned out all the lights and put on the security locks. I packed the stuff I needed in my rucksack and left the office to go home.

Locking the outer door I thought of Billy again. It seemed as though it was the end of our friendship and the fizzling out of any spark of romance we might ever have had.

Boyfriends; it didn't look like I was meant to have one.

6
Second Chance

"I'm not sure I like you getting involved in all this stuff, Patsy, forty-eight." My mum was walking up and down the bottom step of the stairs.

"Tony and I are doing it together," I said. I was cross-legged on the floor looking through my notebook for the address of Second Chance.

"You told me you weren't doing any more crime work, sixty-four," she said, puffing. I wondered how she could talk and exercise at the same time.

"The boy's parents came to see me. Heather Warren sent them. I feel obligated."

"Why do you want to speak to Gerry, seventy-eight?"

"Because he knows all the kids down at Second Chance." I found the right page in my notebook and looked up at my mum. She was wearing a glamorous leotard and leggings. It was one of the new ones she had bought just after she and Gerry got together. She looked thinner than ever, her hair was glowing and she seemed to have a constant, *self-satisfied* smile on her face.

"He said he would be down there about seven. He's coming here later, ninety-two."

"That's nice," I said, not really sure if I meant it or not.

"Ninety-nine, one hundred!"

My mum stopped, her hands on her hips, her breathing becoming slower and slower. After a few seconds she said, "I'm just off to have a shower." I watched her run up the stairs and disappear into the bathroom.

She made me feel tired. Even though I'd taken to doing more walking lately she was still streets ahead of me in the personal fitness race.

I went into the kitchen and put the kettle on. I sat down at the table and thought about my mum's new boyfriend.

In a few weeks Gerry Lawrence had become a fixture in the family. If he wasn't making some toast for himself in the kitchen he was sitting with his feet up in the front room clicking the remote and jumping from one channel to another.

He was pleasant enough to me, I had to admit. He wasn't patronizing like the other couple of men that my mum had spent time with after she and my dad had split up. He treated me like an adult, a house-mate of my mum's rather than her daughter. Instead of fussing over me, like my mum's other boyfriends had, he usually ignored me unless he had something to say.

"Pass us that paper, Pats."

"Got any jam for this toast, Pats?"

"Can you believe what this government is doing, Pats. What do you think?"

Some of the time I quite liked him. I suppose it was because he was so different from the men of his age I had known. My own dad wore a suit when he was working and drove a newish car. My uncle Tony was always dressed up to the nines, constantly worrying about his appearance.

Gerry Lawrence didn't seem to care how he looked. His pot belly sat out over the top of his jeans and his shirt was often unironed, although, I have to say, always clean. He'd been married twice and had two children from different marriages.

He'd become a mature student, although I felt it was a bad description. There was something of the adolescent about Gerry. He had a mischievous look in his eye and held his cigarettes as if he was hiding them from some teacher that was just round the corner. He was all over my mum, as well. A couple of times I'd walked into the front room and found them both in a tight embrace on the settee. My mum had jumped up but Gerry had just sat there, a great smile on his face as if he'd been witnessed having his first ever kiss.

My mum loved the attention. The phone calls and messages left on the answer-phone; the hugs and playful kisses; the bunches of flowers and the walks in the park, down by the river, through the empty city centre. Gerry had even bought her a ring. It was silver and had a big orange stone that looked like a boiled sweet. She wore it whenever they went out, which wasn't often. That was the other thing about Gerry, he never seemed to have any money.

My mum especially seemed to enjoy everyone's disapproval, particularly that of my uncle Tony and aunt Geraldine. Even though I wasn't too sure, in the long run, how good Gerry would be for my mum, I too was gleeful at my uncle's discomfiture and remembered his words, *he's not what you'd call stable*.

Poor uncle Tony. All he wanted was for my mum to meet someone like him.

Before I went out of the front door I checked in the hall mirror to see what I looked like. I'd decided to wear a small hat that my mum had picked up at an attic sale in her college. It was soft maroon and had a small brim on which there was a lot of embroidery. It looked as if some student had bought the hat and customized it.

It looked pretty, although that wasn't a look that I usually aimed for.

Don't get me wrong, I have nothing against looking "pretty" or even "beautiful" if it can be managed. Generally though, me and most of the girls I know don't look like the models in the glossy magazines. We look ordinary, windswept, red-cheeked, overweight, underweight, whatever. Instead of spending years trying to be something I wasn't I tended to go for a particular look. I wore lots of black, jeans, long skirts, my DMs if I felt cold or just for sheer comfort. Mostly, though, I made myself stand out by having a variety of hats to plonk on top of my middling brownish hair. I'd collected them over the years. Some were expensive cast-offs but some were cheap and cheerful, from market stalls and chain stores. Sometimes I gave a plain hat some individual treatment, tacked a bit of chiffon around it or pinned on a velvet flower I'd made.

Once a hat was on my head I looked different, not Patsy Kelly at all, but someone mysterious, interesting.

That was the theory. I pulled the hat down tightly over my skull and went out of the front door.

That's how I looked when I first saw Nathan Dyer.

He was the first person to come over to me when I walked into the Project. He'd been standing next to Gerry Lawrence but walked briskly across the hall and straight up to me.

"Ms Kelly, I believe," he said, holding his hand out. He was staring straight at my hat and I put my hand up, self-consciously, to make sure it was straight. He looked very familiar, as if I had seen him somewhere before.

I looked around, taken aback that someone should know my name. My eye settled on Gerry who was sitting with some young boys over in the corner. He had a broad smile on his face. I put my hand out slowly and Nathan grasped it and shook it confidently.

"Hi…" I said. It had thrown me. I had intended to go briskly into the centre, find the person in charge and then start asking questions.

"Erm…" I added, my hand still in Nathan Dyer's. I had misplaced whatever it was I was going to say.

"You're here about Eddie Wolf," he said, filling in for me. "I'm Nathan. I'm one of the volunteers. The Project leader, Beverley, has just slipped out but I could talk to you, if you like."

"Fine," I said.

Nathan Dyer had his hand lightly on my arm and walked me across the hall towards an office.

"Nath!"

Someone called his name and he stopped. A group of young boys were clustered around a computer terminal.

"I won't be a second," he said and left me standing in the middle of the hall. I took a look around. The space I was in had previously been an assembly hall for some primary school. The fold-away apparatus for gym lessons was still in place and the parquet floor was intact, even though it had accumulated several layers of dust and dirt. There were about twenty or so young people in different groups and half a dozen men. Most of the young people were boys although there were a couple of girls.

There were areas of soft seats screened off from the rest of the hall and some boys were sitting with their legs splayed out, flicking through books. There was an area of tables and a couple of girls were seated there filling out what looked like forms. In the far corner were some bookshelves and filing cabinets and a long line of lockers. One or two were hanging open. There was a sign which hung over the top that said, CAREERS. In the other corner was an area that had several bits of apparatus for weight training. Two girls in track suits were using some of it.

Nathan Dyer was crouched over a computer screen. Then he stood up and was talking to the boys around him. There were four of them all looking at him, a couple speaking, gesticulating, trying to explain something. He stood still, listening to them, concentrating on what they were saying. He seemed to have forgotten about me. He turned back to the screen and then away again, towards me. The boys were looking gratefully at him; there was warmth in their expressions, in the way they stood close to him, in the way one of them patted him on the shoulder, playfully, laughingly.

I found myself looking closely at him. Nathan Dyer was tall, a bit stocky. His hair was long, down past his chin and he had a wide smile, his mouth full to the corners with teeth. As he walked back across the hall towards me I was again struck by a sort of familiarity, as if I'd seen him, or known him somewhere before. His clothes were casual, jeans and a checked shirt. I tried to guess at his age; about nineteen or twenty.

"Computers!" he said, walking briskly. He cupped his hand lightly on my elbow and said, "The office is just over here." I walked along, his touch feeling strange, making my flesh shiver. I was glad when we got to the door of an old classroom and went in.

I sat in one of the soft chairs in a corner, opposite the desk.

"Coffee?" Nathan said.

"Tea, please," I said, crossing and uncrossing my legs, clasping and unclasping my hands.

I told myself I was feeling ill at ease because it was my first real investigation. It was the first time I wasn't working undercover, trying to pretend I was somebody else. I was there legitimately, hired by the boy's parents. I'd just left my confidence in a drawer in the office.

As Nathan handed me my mug of tea I couldn't help but notice that his eyes were hazel, brown with a hint of green.

"Right, Ms Kelly," he said, "or do you mind if I call you Pats? Gerry Lawrence is always talking about you. I feel as if I already know you!"

"No, please," I said, swallowing a whole host of sensible replies. *Pats* sounded entirely different when he said it.

"OK Pats, Eddie Wolf, I knew him quite well, through the centre, you understand. What would you like to know about him?"

"Well," I said, putting my mug of tea on the table, "I'll just get my note pad." In my head there was a voice that was saying *pull yourself together*.

Nathan Dyer leant forward and started to talk. "Eddie Wolf got into trouble with the police about a year ago. Part of his community service order was to attend the Project. He was a nice kid but very impressionable, easily led, you know what I mean?"

I was scribbling some things down, even though I'd heard a lot of this before. It also meant I didn't have to look straight at Nathan Dyer. I couldn't help feeling, though, as I was writing, that he was looking at me.

"I met his dad a couple of times, he came along.

He's a really good bloke. Anyway, Eddie started to come here regularly. He was doing a lot of stuff on the computers and he was also a member of one of the daytime projects, bricklaying and stuff. He joined the Fresh Air Campaign. You probably know that a few of us here are members. I'm not sure how Eddie felt about the issues; I'm not sure he even really understood them. He liked the campaign though, the marches and stuff; like I said, he was easily led."

"Did he have a girlfriend?" I said, trying to get some details that I didn't already know.

"Not really. Between you and me I think he was a bit shy."

I wrote it down, feeling foolishly pleased by his words, *between you and me*, as if he had said this to no one else.

The door opened and Gerry walked in.

"All right, Pats?" he said.

"Yes."

"What's the story, then? I thought Eddie's death was accidental," Gerry said, sitting on one of the soft chairs beside me, immediately lifting his feet up and putting them on the edge of the coffee table.

"It's still unclear," I said. "There's one or two things that aren't really explained. I just need to find out a bit more about him. I need to go and talk to the Fresh Air people."

"There's a meeting tomorrow lunchtime, come to

that," Nathan said.

I found myself picking my mug up and taking a great gulp of lukewarm tea.

"It's at the college at one," Gerry said.

"Nath!" a voice came from outside.

"I'd better go," he said and went out of the door. I sat in silence for a few moments and Gerry walked across to the kettle. I stood up.

"I'll be on my way, then," I said.

"OK, tell your mum I'll see her about ten."

I walked across the hall and took a last look at Nathan Dyer. It came to me who he reminded me of. His long hair and bright smile.

He looked very much like the photo I had of Eddie Wolf.

7
Fresh Air

First thing the next morning I went to see Heather Warren. She was looking even thinner and I noticed that she'd had some blonde highlights put into her hair.

"I'm going to see the campaign group today," I said, "and then to Eddie's house, to look through his things."

"Fair enough," she said. She was packing some papers into a slim tan briefcase that looked new. "I'll tell you what, Patsy, we looked into this case pretty thoroughly. My feeling is that this Georgie Exon feels bad about leaving his friend there. If he'd called an ambulance Eddie might have lived, who knows. He's brooding, looking for a way to explain his friend's death. This story is a way of doing that."

"You don't think Eddie Wolf was looking for something?"

"We searched the whole area. There was nothing unusual. That doesn't mean to say he wasn't looking for something – but what? No, honestly Patsy, I think this is a tragic bit of horseplay that went wrong. Maybe if Georgie Exon gave himself up to the police he'd feel better."

I didn't say anything. I'd heard Georgie Exon's voice on the answer-phone and it had sounded anxious, panicky even. Maybe Heather was right.

"I'll give you a lift to the college," Heather said, putting her jacket on. "I'm going that way."

"Thanks," I said, sighing. The truth was I didn't have much enthusiasm for going to the Fresh Air meeting but I felt I had to go through the motions. It was important to Mr and Mrs Wolf.

Heather was driving her own car. It was raining heavily and I was glad I had brought a hat.

"Are you off duty?" I said. We were moving slowly along, the traffic bumper to bumper along the High Street. The rain was glittering on the windscreen, like hundreds of tiny jewels.

"Not exactly, I'm going to meet some women colleagues. We're putting together a support group for women in the force."

I noticed a small NO SMOKING PLEASE! sign on Heather's dashboard. I wondered when she had given up.

"WPCs are wickedly discriminated against. You just look around, Patsy, how many women are in top jobs in the police?"

I found myself looking round, out on to the street, at the car in front. I didn't bother mentioning that she was one of the youngest detective inspectors in the force and that several older men, like my uncle Tony, had found her promotion galling. She was right, though. Unless you were outstanding, like her, you didn't stand a chance.

The rain was streaking down the passenger window making the street outside look blurred. There were people ducking under umbrellas and sheltering under shop canopies and in doorways. Right in the middle of the pavement, next to a bus stop, a solitary individual was standing, his collar turned up, seemingly oblivious to the downpour. It was Gerry Lawrence.

I could hear Heather humming a tune as I wound down the window.

"Gerry!" I shouted. "It's the man from the Fresh Air Campaign. The one I'm meeting today."

"Get him to jump in. He can have a lift," Heather said, pulling over to the pavement. I motioned to Gerry who came hurriedly across. I got out of the car and felt the rain pricking on to my face and my glasses. I lifted the seat and Gerry climbed into the back of the car.

"Heather, this is Gerry Lawrence. He's in the

Fresh Air Campaign that I told you about."

Gerry's hair was dripping with water and his glasses were splattered. He was in his old denim jacket and jeans, his portly figure peeping out above the waistband. He had a big smile on his face and was making no effort to dry himself.

"Hello," Heather said.

"Gerry's a mature student," I added. I decided not to add that he was my mum's boyfriend.

"Heather's a detective inspector," I said, trying to make some conversation.

"Ah," Gerry said, "one of the girls in blue."

"What are you studying?" Heather said, turning around slightly when we had stopped at lights.

"History," Gerry said. "I'm looking at social history. Lots about the law enforcers in that."

I looked at Heather, hoping she wasn't offended by Gerry's flippant tone. She was giving him an odd look.

I turned back, wondering whether Gerry had perhaps had some dealings with the police in the past. Twice divorced, unemployed, always involved in campaigns for this and that. Maybe Gerry had a record.

We arrived at the college a couple of minutes later.

"Thanks, Heather," I said, when Gerry had got out.

"Take care, Patsy," she said, but she seemed to be looking past me, her eyes on Gerry. I wondered then whether she remembered him from some line-up or from a picture in a book of mug shots.

It wouldn't have surprised me.

The meeting room was a small study room off the main corridor of the college. There were about thirty people in there, mostly younger students but some older ones, like Gerry. I looked round to see if Nathan Dyer was there. He wasn't and I couldn't help but feel disappointed.

There were posters everywhere about the demonstration on Saturday. *DEFEND THE AIR! STOP THE KILLER ROADS.*

The main speaker was standing behind a wooden podium. She was a young woman with giant glasses and a hippie-type floral dress. When she turned to speak to someone behind her I noticed that her hair fell heavily down to her waist. I immediately felt envious. It was the kind of hair that hadn't been cut since childhood. I fingered my own locks curling round my neck and thought, for a moment, about the little piles of hair that had sat on the floors of a dozen hairdresser's shops over the years, only to be swept aside and bagged up for the bin men.

I pulled my gaze away and saw Gerry Lawrence sitting behind her with a couple of other people talking quietly behind their hands. After a few seconds she banged the podium and started to talk.

"I want to talk to you today about why Fresh Air

was formed, about who we are and what we stand for." Her voice was quivering slightly.

There were a few coughs and the door opened, admitting some latecomers. One of them was Nathan. I turned away, avoiding, for some reason, looking directly at him.

"The proliferation of road building in the last ten years has been caused by the total domination of the individual car as a means of transport. By the year 2000 there will be millions more cars on the roads. Millions.

"Can you imagine that?"

She stopped for a minute and looked around the audience. I found myself thinking about her question. I had an image of a world of giant motorways, twenty lanes across, criss-crossing the country; cars and lorries screaming along, bypassing tiny towns that sat under thick clouds of polluted air; people walking along, dwarfed by rows of powerful vehicles.

I remembered Billy's words; *handled sensibly, the motor car is a modern miracle*.

Using one of her hands to sweep her hair back she went on, "We're not against progress. We're not against the car. The road builders say that there are too many cars so we have to build more roads. We say if there are too many cars then we should cut down on our use of them, not cover the country with tarmac.

"But how do we cut down on cars?"

I imagined Billy sitting listening to the talk with his lips curling, his arms crossed in silent resignation, his foot tapping with irritation.

"We build a better public transport system. We have twice as many buses and trains and tubes than are running at present and we cut the price of using them by half. In a stroke it would cut the use of the motor car."

There was a mumble of agreement and even though I wasn't strictly there for the talk I found myself nodding my head. I looked across the room and saw Nathan smiling at me. I smiled back and then felt silly. I got my notebook out and tried to force myself to think about the reason that I was there. The speaker continued and I began to take notes on the group, the talk, the room, anything to stop myself feeling self-conscious in front of Nathan Dyer.

"The demonstration on Saturday is an important tool for raising public awareness on this issue and that's why I want each and every one of you to bring your friends and your family along.

"There has been talk about violence on the demonstrations and I understand that there will be a large police presence on Saturday. Please do not be put off by this. We do not seek violence out." She stopped, her eyes closed for a moment, her voice a little shaky. I looked around and saw several other people looking into their laps, one or two shaking their heads. Eddie Wolf had been a friend of theirs. It was understandable that they should still be upset by his death. The woman continued, "We do not seek violence out but if, in the end, it is the only way to make the public take notice then we will not shy away." Her voice had risen, full of emotion. "We will fight if we have to!" There was a brief handclap.

"We will assemble at the town hall and people should carry as many banners as they can make. The more noise and colour we create the more notice we will get."

She stood back and Gerry was immediately on his feet with his hand on her arm. There was a low murmuring and people began to get up off their seats and walk towards her. I moved in that direction myself, drifting along with the crowd, not sure where to go or who to talk to.

Just then I found Nathan at my elbow.

"Pats," he said, "you look a bit lost. What did you think of Beverley's talk?"

"Really interesting," I said, being honest.

"She's the Project leader at Second Chance. Amazing character. Really nice woman."

"Yes," I said. His hand was on the underside of my arm, warm and firm and my skin was tingling.

"Here," he said, "I'll introduce you to some of Eddie Wolf's friends. Sarah and Joanne, he was quite pally with them."

I felt him pull me in the direction of a couple of girls who were sitting in a corner. He introduced me and I stood there awkwardly, not knowing quite what to say.

"Pats is working for Eddie's mum and dad," Nathan said, pulling his hair back into an elastic band.

"Really?" one of the girls said, her eyes glued to Nathan's face. Her friend was the same, only flicking her eyes at me and then honing back in his direction. It was disconcerting.

After a minute Nathan left me with them and went to talk to another dark haired girl with a ring through her nose. Sarah and Joanne looked narrow-eyed in her direction. I was interested myself but I pulled my attention back to the matter in hand. In a kind of detached way I started to talk to them about Eddie Wolf. How long had they known him, who was he friendly with, what was he like, what about Georgie Exon, etc.

I wrote their answers down but I wasn't really listening to them. My attention, along with theirs, seemed to be straying to the part of the room where Nathan was.

Eddie was all right, wasn't he, Jo? He was friendly like, a bit hot-headed, we were shocked when we heard about the accident, but he was a bit of a devil, taking chances and stuff. He came here after he got done for some burglary, I think. His probation officer was that

Cheryl, you know, the big woman with the funny glasses.

I scribbled along, my mind wandering until I finally lost track of what they both were saying. The dark haired girl that Nathan was talking to was looking across at me, her expression serious. I wondered, for a moment, whether it was his girlfriend. I felt a pang of dismay. I hadn't thought about him being attached to someone. I turned back to my pad and copied down a couple of last comments.

He didn't have a girlfriend, he was shy was our Eddie.

I looked around after placing my final full stop and realized that Nathan and the dark haired girl had both gone. Gerry was waving at me to come over and talk to some more people. I said thanks to Joanne and Sarah and walked, my feet like lead, over to Gerry.

I left about twenty minutes later. The pages of my pad were covered with little notes, most of which I thought would probably be useless. Eddie Wolf had been dead for almost four weeks and already his personality had become bland, just like any young hot-headed teenager.

I began to feel frustrated. If Georgie Exon were to come forward the whole thing could be cleared up. This way, Mr and Mrs Wolf were wasting their hard earned cash on a fruitless enquiry which would probably yield nothing.

I was pulling my jacket around me when I heard someone's voice.

"Pats!"

I looked round and saw the dark haired girl, the one I had thought was Nathan's girlfriend, in the doorway of a classroom. She was looking round as well, as though she was afraid of anyone seeing her.

"Pats," she said again. I walked over to her.

"Yes?" I said, looking at my watch. I'd had enough of the college and the Fresh Air Campaign.

"I got something I think I should tell you."

I felt myself stand up straight. "I'm sorry, I didn't catch your name..." I started.

"No, no names. And I don't want no one to know I told you this. I'll deny it if you do."

"OK," I said, my hand in mid-air. I found myself looking up and down the corridor.

"Something happened a while ago. I didn't think anything about it, you know, but I'm not so sure now." She looked round, worried, cross with herself. I edged past her and pulled the classroom door closed. I sat on the edge of a desk but she stood, uneasily, by the door.

"A week or so before he died, I saw Eddie. It was late at night. He was sitting in the front seat of this flash car. It was up near the forest. I was walking my dog. I'm sure it was a Mercedes or something like that. The registration was half covered but I saw the first three letters REM. I was going to wave, you know, until I saw the car. I didn't though. I just stood across the road, in the dark I was. He was talking to some older man. Eventually he got out and waved and the car pulled out. I went over to him, I thought he had a rich uncle or something. He had his back to me. I patted him on the shoulder and he jumped, you know, like I was a ghost."

I listened. She was weaving her fingers together, her forehead creased. I noticed on her arm a tattoo of a flower.

"He turned round to me and dropped all this money. It flew out of his hand. Fivers, tenners, there must have been about twenty of them. I said to him, you won the lottery or what? He said, no, no I was just meeting my dad, he gives me some money now and then. I didn't know him that well then, see. I thought his dad really was well off. He told me not to say anything to anyone. He didn't want anyone to know that his family were rich. I didn't say anything to the police or anything because I didn't think it was relevant but then, the other day, Eddie's mum and dad came to a meeting, you know to talk about him. I could see they weren't well off. I could see he'd been lying."

I got my notebook out.

"What you writing down?" she said, looking fearful.

"Just the registration, that's all." I wrote REM in my book and put it away.

"Don't put my name," she said.

"I don't know it," I smiled.

"I've got to go," she said and walked out of the door. I heard her footsteps running off down the corridor, hurrying as if I might chase after her.

Why was she so afraid of me?

I walked out of the classroom and along the corridor to the exit. I felt a tiny prod of excitement. Eddie Wolf had taken money from a well-off man in a car, late at night and had lied about it. I wondered what it meant.

I came out of the main doors and saw, in the distance, Nathan Dyer and the girl I'd just been talking to. It was clear that they were arguing, indeed Nathan was holding her arm and she was looking spitefully at him. When he saw me he let go and looked embarrassed. The girl turned her back and walked away and he followed after her.

Were they involved with each other? It certainly looked like it. I clicked my tongue in resignation and went back to thinking about Eddie Wolf. The teen-ager who had broken the law but was making up for it with Second Chance. The young, good-looking lad who everyone liked. The daredevil campaigner who had died in a tragic accident.

The boy in the Mercedes taking money from some unspecified source.

It was what they called a lead.

I was grateful.

8
Search

Back at the office I swapped information with my uncle Tony. He had been down to the building site as well as to the old security firm that was on duty at the time of Eddie's death. He had checked over the statements that the building workers had made and had a look around the derelict houses that Eddie had, according to Georgie Exon, been searching in.

He was very interested in my story about Eddie getting out of the car, late at night, with a fistful of money.

"Perhaps he was still involved in burglary? Selling stolen goods," Tony said, looking at me over the rim of a mug of tea.

"Unlikely," I said. "It's not the way stolen goods get sold, is it?"

"Depends what it is," he said. "If it were small expensive pieces of jewellery, diamonds, set pieces…"

"But how would Eddie Wolf have access to those?"

"What was he arrested for? House burglary?"

We went on like that for a while, batting the details back and forth, not really getting anywhere. There was an edge to my uncle's voice, as if he were suspicious of the things that I had found out. He was on one side of his desk and I was on the other. For the first time, ever, I think, he was forced into talking to me as an equal. I was no longer his difficult niece or the clerical worker that had been pushed on him by my mother. I don't think he found it easy.

It was a murder case, though. The first he had handled in years and he was secretly thrilled, I think. I imagined him walking round the building site, holding his jacket over his shoulder by the tag, a note pad in his other hand, a pencil behind his ear.

After a while we made some fresh plans. I wrote them down and read them out.

"You're going to check out the registration number of the car. There can't be that many Mercedes with the registration REM. You're also going to see Eddie's old probation officer, Cheryl Spenser. I'm going over to Eddie's house to look through his things. Although I'm sure the police will have tried already," I said.

"Maybe," Tony said, "but they weren't really looking for anything specific."

"That's true," I said, thoughtfully.

Tony was right, for once. We were looking at Eddie in a new light. Maybe there would be something in his belongings that would give some kind of explanation.

Mrs Wolf took me straight up to Eddie's bedroom. She seemed very different from the day I'd met her in Tony's office. She was in a turquoise tracksuit, her pink hair tied back in a matching band. On her feet she wore trainers. Altogether she looked more chunky, more at ease. I noticed that her face looked tired, though. She couldn't have been much older than my mum but she looked weary, deep lines in her forehead. I wondered if she was sleeping. I followed her into the room.

"I've cleared the room up, I'm afraid. The police didn't seem interested, you know, so I tidied a bit…"

It looked like a young boy's bedroom. There were football pictures on the walls and models of cars and motorbikes on the window-sill. There was an Action Man on a stand on top of a chest of drawers, beside him a model size truck. The shelf in the corner was covered in soft toys, one of them, a cheeky looking gorilla that looked very like one that I had, tucked away in a bottom drawer, under my

Sindy doll and my toy cooker. The duvet had a Superman design on it which matched the lamp-shade on the bedside light.

It was a room for a boy of about ten. I noticed a small bookcase on the other side of the bed. Some of the titles were familiar – *The Lion, the Witch and the Wardrobe, Treasure Island, The Diary of Adrian Mole*, some Terry Pratchett books, even a copy of an Enid Blyton book, *Five on an Island*.

"We always bought him lots of books," Mrs Wolf said.

I had almost forgotten she was there. I looked round and her eyes had glassed over. I went to put my hand out but she seemed to straighten up and move back towards the door.

"I'll make some tea," she said.

"Two sugars, a dash of milk," I said, to cover the embarrassment.

Then she was gone.

I sat down on the bed. The duvet sank slowly under me. It was a while since anyone had slept there. It was certainly some time since the room had looked like this. I realized that the search was going to be useless. Mrs Wolf had either discarded or put away many of her son's grown-up things.

I pulled open some of the drawers and saw piles of neatly ironed clothes. I opened the small wardrobe and saw trousers and jackets hanging uniformly in a row. Underneath there were pairs of shoes and trainers lined up side by side. A single school tie hung on a rack on the back of the door.

I sat down again and looked around the room. Where was the hi-fi? The computer? The piles of junk that teenagers amass?

It was gone.

The door opened and she came in with a single mug of tea.

"Here," she said.

I took the mug and put it down on the bedside table.

"What happened to Eddie's things?" I said, more abruptly than I meant to.

She looked round the room for a moment. Then she sat on the bed.

"You have to understand, Patricia, for the last few years my Eddie wasn't really like a son to me. He was a grown-up, a lad, someone I hardly recognized. He stole from other people's houses, he got into trouble, he brought the police to this house. The first time ever. For a while, when Cheryl was looking after him, we thought he'd come through it all, that he'd changed."

I didn't speak.

"When he died, I wanted rid of all those things, the loud music, the shabby clothes, the frayed jeans, the posters of ugly, angry young men and women. I wanted them all out. I piled them all into a black plastic bag and took them down to the council dump. I would have burned them but Les wouldn't let me.

"I decided that I wanted the room to stay as it was when Eddie was younger."

The door closed behind her and I was left on my own in a bedroom which had gone back in time.

I got up and went over to the bookcase. There were some small photos in ornate stands. They were school portraits of Eddie taken at different ages. The first was when he was very young, five or six, I thought. The next two were interchangeable. He had a heavy fringe and a giant smile. There were one or two teeth missing as well. The next was when he was about eleven. His hair had been cut very short and he only had the hint of a smile. How different he looked. I remembered his mum's words – *he was a grown-up, someone I hardly recognized*.

I drank the last of my tea and was about to go when I was drawn back to the books. They were all paperbacks except for one, *Treasure Island*. It was dark brown and bigger than the rest. I remembered being forced to read it in senior school. I reached over and picked it out. I placed my empty mug on top of the bookcase and opened it, expecting to see hundreds of pages of dreary close print.

A key dropped out.

At first I wasn't exactly sure what it was because it fell past my hands, hitting my leg, then on to the floor.

A small silver key. I bent down and picked it up. I held the book upside down by its hard cover, to see if anything else was there but there was nothing.

I looked carefully over the key for a number or any indication of what it might belong to. It was plain, though, and it reminded me of the locker keys at school. Everyone had made such a fuss to get lockers and when they were installed no one wanted to use them.

A locker key. I held it up remembering the lockers at Second Chance. I wondered if Eddie had had one there.

I looked at my watch and decided to go there on my way home.

9
Discovery

It was six o'clock when I got to Second Chance. The place was empty, only a couple of boys hanging around the front door. I walked past them and into the big hall. Over in the corner, I could see Nathan's back. In his hand he had a broom and was sweeping the floor. He looked round and smiled. I walked across to him.

"Hi," he said. "How did you enjoy the Fresh Air meeting?"

"Oh," I said, truthfully, "yes, it was impressive."

"Did you find out anything, about Eddie?" he said, looking so closely at me that I had to look away. I wondered again about the girl with the tattoo.

"Just background," I said, glancing over at the far wall where I had seen the lockers, "nothing earth shattering." I had decided, with Tony's advice, to keep any information I got to myself.

"Maybe that's it with Eddie," he said, shrugging his shoulders.

"Yes, you're probably right. There is one thing, though. I wondered if Eddie might have had a locker or something here," I said, pointing over to the row of dishevelled lockers on the far wall.

He looked puzzled for a moment.

"You mean, one of those? I shouldn't think so."

He walked over to them and I followed. As we got closer I realized that we were going to find nothing. Most of them were swinging open, a few had no door at all. A couple were shut over but the handle and the lock had been removed. I felt foolish.

"Could I look in them anyway?"

"Sure," he said. "I honestly don't think anyone actually uses them. Dusty old things."

I made a show of squatting down and peering into the dark corners of the old lockers. I opened a couple of others while he stood behind me. All the time I felt his eyes on my back. At one point I stood up hurriedly and backed into him.

"Whoops," he said.

"Sorry," I said, feeling his hands on the backs of my shoulders. I closed my eyes at my own stupidity and then turned round to find myself face to face with him. He pushed the front of his hair back and I took a step backwards, feeling all the time that he was holding on to me with a look that was impossible to read.

"Tell you what," he said, his hand touching my arm for a minisecond, "I'll just lock up, then I'll put the kettle on, shall I?"

"Yes," I said and watched him as he walked away, his footsteps echoing in the empty hall towards the office.

I turned back to the lockers even though I was no longer looking at them. I felt the skin on my arm that he had touched a minute before.

What was it about him that struck me so much? That made me go weak in the legs?

I didn't know. I closed my eyes, turned around and walked towards the office.

After we finished the tea he started to talk about himself. We were on two soft chairs near the window. It was still light outside but the blinds were partly down and the room was in shadow. The desk lamp was the only light that was on. From where I was sitting it looked like a candle, glowing in the dusk.

"I finished my GCSEs about two, three years ago. I didn't fancy college. I'd had enough of studying, the real truth is I wasn't that bright." He was pointing to his head with his hand. "I tried to get a job, for months I tried. I worked in a butcher's for a while, apprentice, but I couldn't take the meat. All that blood. Then there was the factory job, packing up boxes of sliced loaves for Sainsbury's. I thought I was going to go mad. Butcher, baker, soldier, sailor. In the end..."

He stopped speaking and then leant forward again, as though he was about to whisper something secret in my ear.

"Between you and me," he said, and I felt his hot breath on the side of my face, "between you and me, I don't think I'm cut out to hold a job down."

"You're a volunteer here, then?" I said, my voice quivering, noticing that he hadn't moved back away from me.

"I am," he was whispering and I felt his fingers playing with a strand of my hair. I held my breath. I thought that at any moment he was going to lean over and kiss me.

Then he did.

I hadn't realized how much I had wanted him to. The skin on my neck and chest was tingling as he put his hand behind my head and pulled my face towards his. He kissed me on the mouth, not softly or nervously but deliberately. In the dark of the room I closed my eyes and tasted him, soft and wet against my lips. Somewhere, far away in the back of my head was a voice saying, *What do you think you're doing?*

A knocking broke the silence.

In the twilight of the room we both moved back,

the moment disintegrating. We stood up, looking guiltily at each other.

"I wonder who that is," he said, regaining his smile. He walked across the room and out of the door. I looked round at the office; it no longer seemed so dark, so quiet, Nathan's footsteps sounding from one corner of the building to the other.

For a few seconds I stood with my fingers on my lips, mesmerized by what had happened. Then I shook myself, remembering why I was there, what I was supposed to be looking for.

There was a light switch by an open door that led into a smaller room. I clicked it on and saw that it was a staff toilet and washroom. I noticed the line of aluminium lockers in there. About six of them, side by side against the wall. I looked at them for a few seconds until Nathan came running back across the floor of the hall.

"It's Bev," he said, out of breath, "she wants me to help her unpack some stuff from her car. I'll only be a minute. Hang around, you can talk to her. She's really nice."

"OK," I said. I had already talked to Beverley briefly at the Fresh Air meeting. She hadn't been able to tell me much that was new about Eddie. I looked at the lockers again and wondered how long it would be before they came back in.

I picked up my jacket. My hands were trembling as I searched deep into my pockets and found the key. In a mad rush I tried the lockers one after the other. The key fitted the second to last locker.

I sat back a minute, not knowing whether to open it or not. Was it right to pry into people's privacy without their permission? I only had to wait a few minutes before Nathan and Beverley came in. I could ask them then.

I found myself nodding in agreement with these proper thoughts but my hand had turned the key anyway and a second or so later the door was open.

There was only one thing inside.

A small cardboard shoe box with the words *Hands off Eddies* scribbled in thick felt-tip. From the back of my head I could hear voices in the distance. They sounded a long way off but in a few moments I knew that Nathan and Beverley would be here, curious, cross even, that I had been searching without permission.

I picked up the box and closed the locker door quietly. I got my rucksack from the chair and fitted the box awkwardly inside it. The voices were coming nearer and I lay my jacket over the rucksack and held the whole thing in my hands.

The door opened and Beverley came in carrying a cardboard box that said UHT Longlife Milk on the outside.

"Hello," she said, uncertainly.

"Hi," I said, as Nathan followed her in, carrying a giant see-through bag of white polystyrene cups.

"We met yesterday. Nathan's just been chatting to me. I had some of your tea, I hope you don't mind." The words came tumbling out in a pile up.

"Not at all," she said, turning round to put the box down on the desk.

Her hair was in a single plait that reached right down to her waist. It held my attention for a few seconds and then I saw her looking at the bulging rucksack that was bundled up in my arms.

"I do have to run, Nathan. Maybe I could come and speak to you some other time?" I said, looking at Beverley.

"Of course, anytime," she said.

"I'll give you a ring, Patsy," Nathan said.

I found myself smiling stupidly and left the room. I was conscious of my protruding belongings and made myself walk across the parquet floor instead of running. Once out of the main doors I walked quickly in the direction of the bus stop.

It was only when I'd paid my fare that I began to wonder about the door of the locker. Had I locked it again? I couldn't remember. I tucked it to the back of my mind and all the way home I thought about Nathan Dyer and the kiss.

10
The Lives of Eddie Wolf

The contents of the box lay on my bed. I was sitting cross-legged, my glasses pushed back on top of my head, looking closely at the objects.

There was a valentine card, a big one with a red satin heart on the front. There was no name inside, just a couple of kisses, scrawled roughly across the middle of the page. I held it up to my nose and it smelt of sickly sweet talcum powder.

A paperback book lay to the side. It was a battered copy of *Love Poetry*. I flicked through the pages again. Some old poems, right back to Shakespeare, but a lot of new stuff that didn't rhyme and had uneven length lines. English never had been my best subject at school. Inside the cover were the words, *Eddie, I hope you like this*, printed in minuscule letters.

A Rolex-type watch, a fake probably, and a pair of costume earrings, big glittering maroon stones in a silver surround. I wondered if they were a present for the sender of the valentine card.

Then there was the money. A roll of twenty pound notes, held together by a thick elastic band doubled over. I pulled it off carefully and the notes lay, still curled up, about twenty of them. Four hundred pounds.

Eddie Wolf was becoming more mysterious by the minute. There seemed to be a number of personalities emerging. One, the smiling mischievous campaigner, retraining, taking a second chance in life. Another was a shady person who took money from mysterious men in cars late at night. The third was Eddie in love, involved in a secret liaison. It had been going on for some time judging by the fact that it was almost four months since Valentine's Day.

In love.

I sat back on the bed for a few moments and Nathan Dyer came into my head. It didn't take much effort for me to push thoughts of Eddie Wolf aside and think of the kiss he and I had had. A shiver went through my chest and I remembered his fingers on my hair, his voice whispering in my ear. I let myself imagine his arms around me, his hands rubbing up and down my back and the touch of his skin on my face and neck.

What was it about him that struck me so forcefully? The girl with the tattoo came into my head again. Had they been involved, in the past maybe?

I thought about Billy for a moment and felt a tiny prick of guilt. The romance between him and me had always seemed to be simmering gently on the back burner. Now, in two days I had bubbles inside my chest every time I thought about Nathan.

I purposely let out a long sigh, stretched out my feet and dislodged a few of the twenty pound notes. I looked at the items on the bed with mild annoyance; they were diversions, pulling me out of the romantic reverie I was in.

I sat up again, feeling weary, wondering what it all meant.

The honest truth was I had lost interest in the case. Or at least, my concern for the case was being submerged in my interest in Nathan Dyer. It was like a novel that I had started to read grudgingly when a better one had come along. I was trying to read them both together and it wasn't working. I needed to prioritize.

I got up off the bed, and got an old sketch pad from the shelf. In the middle I wearily drew a circle and wrote the words *Eddie Wolf*. Around the circle I drew lines so that it looked like a sun that a small child might draw. At the end of the lines I wrote all the different things I knew about Eddie so far. I did it randomly, mixing up the details in the hope that some link might show up.

Eddie in love ended up next to *seen by tattoo girl in car late at night*. Had the girl with the tattoo been involved with Eddie and not Nathan, after all? It was a possibility. Next to *on probation* was George Exon's name. I began to wonder how George Exon and Eddie had got to know each other. Was it through Fresh Air or Second Chance? Or had they known each other before, in the days when Eddie had been in trouble with the police?

I was beginning to get quite interested in the whole puzzle again when I heard the phone ringing. After a couple of seconds my mum called up to me.

"Pat, it's for you! Nathan someone."

I skipped along the hall and took the call on my mum's bedside phone. When I picked up the receiver I realized that I had my sun diagram with me. I propped it up against the phone, took a deep breath and said, "Hello."

"Hi, Pats. You rushed off tonight!" he said.

I felt myself stuttering, "I had some things to do."

"About the case?" His voice was cheerful. I felt my spirits rising.

"Yes, just one or two loose ends to follow up." I looked at the diagram and realized that I hadn't included Nathan's name; I scribbled it down.

"Look, something's come up, about what happened to Eddie. I can't say if it amounts to anything because I'm not really sure of the facts."

"Really?" I said, puzzled.

"I heard this story from some kids in the group which I never really took much notice of. It didn't really occur to me to tell you, but Gerry mentioned it tonight. Number 82, that's the middle house that's still standing, had this very old guy living there. He was one of the residents that said he wouldn't move, no matter what. He was eighty-something and in the end I think he died. You still there?"

"Yes," I said. I was sitting on my mum's bed, fiddling with the phone wire.

"A couple of the younger ones who talked to the old guy, Albert, Albie I think his name was, they said that he used to boast about keeping his valuables in a tin box under the floor, safe from burglars he said. The old boy apparently went on about having been much richer as a young man and possessing masses of jewellery."

"Jewellery?" I said, thinking of the paste earrings I had found inside Eddie's box.

"Yes, I mean it's just rumours, which is why no one's bothered to tell the police."

"But it could be true."

"That's what I thought. We could go and look, if you like."

"Go and look? How?"

"The security guards have eased up in the last couple of weeks. I even heard they'd laid a few of them off. The thing is we have a number of ways of getting on to the site that nobody knows about. I'm not really supposed to tell anyone about it, not even you but..."

He didn't finish the sentence. I butted in.

"It would be brilliant if we could go and look," I said, my mind racing ahead with all sorts of possibilities.

"OK. It would have to be tonight, later, about eleven."

"Eleven?" I repeated, beginning to feel a bit apprehensive.

"There's a changeover of shifts then and the guards chat for a few minutes. It's a distraction for them. It'll give us enough time to get in without being seen."

I was quiet for a minute.

"Are you still there?" he said.

"Yes," I said. What was the harm in going? If I found some valuables it might at least corroborate what Georgie Exon had said and the police would have to become more involved.

"Are you coming?" he said.

"Yes," I said, woodenly. Was I going to have the courage to break into a forbidden area where there were guards and very possibly dogs?

"I thought we'd do it together," he said, "just you and me. We'll make a good team."

That was it. If he'd asked me to break into the

Bank of England I'd have gone. He spent a few minutes telling me how they got into the site and where to meet him. I put the phone down feeling exhilarated. Whether it was because of the investigation I was going on or just Nathan's company I couldn't have said. I picked up my diagram and went back to my room.

I had a long shower, standing for ages letting the water soak through me. I wanted to wake myself up. I had my cassette player on the hall landing, playing music loudly enough for me to hear above the shower. My mum had gone out for the evening so I didn't have to worry about her tearing up the stairs and turning the volume down. I decided that I would leave her a note to say that I would be in much later and for her not to wait up for me.

I dressed completely in black and found a close fitting woolly hat to put over my hair. I had decided to leave my glasses off. It wasn't vanity or anything like that, I just thought they'd get in the way.

Looking at myself in the mirror was a bit of a shock. I looked like some kind of soldier about to parachute behind enemy lines. I began to feel worried again. It was a foolhardy thing to do. We might get caught; we could get hurt. I took the hat off and sat down on the bed and looked at the box with *Hands off Eddies* written on it.

I remembered another time when I'd gone into a

dark, derelict house by myself. I'd almost been killed and been lectured then about not doing things on my own.

I had to be sensible. After a few minutes indecision I decided to ring Tony and get his advice.

He was out. My aunt Geraldine said that he wouldn't be back until very late. As I replaced the receiver I noticed the answer-phone light blinking on and off. Someone must have rung while I was in the shower. I pressed the play button. It was Tony. In the background I could hear a lot of voices and the faint sounds of music. I guessed that he was calling from a pub.

"Patricia, I've spent a bit of time with Cheryl Spenser, Eddie's probation officer. I'll fill you in tomorrow about it. As well as that, Pete, my old contact at the station, has found the registration number for me. M254 REM, a blue Mercedes. It's owned by Ronald Mitchell, otherwise known as the managing director of SAFECO. By coincidence, the other place they look after is the construction site of the new shopping centre. Where Les Wolf works. We'll talk more tomorrow. Strategy meeting, nine o'clock, in the office."

I grabbed a piece of paper and listened to it again, making a note of the important bits.

Ronald Mitchell was involved. Giving Eddie Wolf money.

I looked at my watch. It was time to leave and I hadn't been able to talk to Tony. I picked up my rucksack, took a deep breath and went out into the dark night.

11
Nathan Dyer

I got to the place where Nathan had said we would meet. I had decided to try and persuade him not to go on the site but to come to the police with me the next morning. The house could then be searched in daylight. It made much more sense. It wasn't nearly as adventurous or romantic but it was the smart thing to do. That's what I told myself.

I was early so I wandered along to the High Street and thought about getting a bag of chips. I hummed and hawed for a few minutes smelling the vinegar from the shop but then decided against it. It might look as though I wasn't taking the case seriously.

As I walked back I thought about the things my uncle had said.

The Mercedes with the registration REM

belonged to Ronald Mitchell the head of SAFECO, the new security company that had taken over the site after Eddie Wolf's death.

A Mercedes car came into my head. It was parked close to the giant diggers and the rubble from the link site. Beside it was a man in a grey suit, trying to fit a yellow safety helmet on to his head. He'd looked funny, out of place in his smart clothes, as if he were more at home in a boardroom than a building site. I had seen him only the previous day when I'd been walking past the link road. Had that been Ronald Mitchell? I had no way of knowing.

I walked on and in my head I constructed a possible train of events. SAFECO was a local security company who specialized in looking after building sites. The only work they had had was the site at the new shopping centre, where, incidentally, Eddie's dad worked as a foreman. Perhaps they knew each other, this Ronald Mitchell and Les Wolf, only in passing. Maybe Eddie himself had been at the site to meet his dad or even to do some casual labouring. Somehow Ronald had heard about Eddie's past and the fact that he had joined the Fresh Air Campaign.

The contract for looking after the new road site was a lucrative one. It would mean months, maybe years, of guaranteed work. SAFECO hadn't got the contract, though. What if Ronald Mitchell started to try and discredit the other security company? He may have contacted Eddie and offered him money to disrupt the building process. It was true that Eddie had been involved in a number of escapades in the weeks leading up to his death. There were more demonstrations and Eddie had been one of the people who had chained himself to a tree. That whole business had stopped work on the road for three or four days.

Eddie was on the brink of tampering with the machines on the night he died. That would have meant more delays.

Would SAFECO have stood a good chance then of getting the contract?

Meanwhile Eddie had been found dead.

Had someone in the Fresh Air Campaign found out about Eddie taking money? Had the girl with the tattoo told anyone else? She had looked particularly jumpy when talking to me.

Had someone killed him because he had been a "traitor"?

Another thought occurred to me that was equally unpleasant.

Had Ronald Mitchell had Eddie killed so that the ensuing uproar about the lack of security would ensure that he got the contract?

I was back at the spot where I said I would meet Nathan. I leant against a wall and pondered the question. Were these things – loyalty, contracts, money – were they really a matter of life and death?

I didn't bother to try and answer it. I knew from my involvement in other murders that people kill and get killed for what seems like the flimsiest of reasons. I waited in the dark street, my breath forming small clouds in the cold spring night air and wished, more than anything, that I had bought that bag of chips.

When Nathan was ten minutes late I began to worry.

Ten-forty-five he had said we'd meet. On the corner of Lester Avenue, a couple of streets away from the site. I was sure he'd said that. I kept thinking of his words: *Some of the fencing is weak along the back of the housing between the tube line and the site. We just have to walk along beside the track for a few seconds then duck through the wire netting and we're in.*

The tube line. That hadn't sunk in when he'd first said it. He was planning to walk along by the side of an *electric* track. I shook my head and looked at my watch again.

Nathan had said ten-forty-five. I was sure of that. Or was I?

I began to worry that during my brief walk up to the chip shop and back Nathan had come along and not seeing me there had gone on to the site himself. I didn't know what to do. I walked twenty metres along to the next road to see if, by mistake, he was waiting there. There was no sign of him, though.

I was sure he wouldn't let me down. I didn't allow myself even to contemplate it. He had come early and gone on without me. Perhaps he thought that I wasn't coming, had got cold feet.

It was getting close to eleven, the time when the security guard shifts would change. Soon it would be too late to go into the site.

I stood, filled with indecision. I didn't know what to do. If he had gone on on his own he may well be in danger, he may get caught and arrested. At least if I was there with him I could explain what we were doing. There was a sound of approaching voices and I half hoped one of them was Nathan's, that he had changed his mind and was coming to meet me to go for a late drink. The voices passed by, though – two teenagers, lighting cigarettes behind cupped hands, their faces lit up for a second and then merging back into the darkness.

I had a choice. I either had to go in and see if he was there or go home.

I found the opening to the tube track quite quickly, just where Nathan had said it would be. It was about five metres from the big sign that said, LONDON TRANSPORT. BEWARE 5000 VOLTS. TRESPASSERS WILL BE PROSECUTED. The fencing had been weakened by an impact, perhaps a car or lorry had crashed into it. It was still standing in place but not joined on to the next section. I pushed it gently and it moved back about twenty centimetres. I turned sideways and slid through. I found myself on a strip of grass that was about six metres away from the track itself. In the distance I could see the lights of the station; I could even make out a few people standing waiting for a train on the platform.

I walked along the fencing for about ten metres and behind it I could see the old derelict houses on the road site loom up in the darkness. Nathan had said the fencing was weak somewhere around there. The whole area was thick with shrubs and bushes so I got my torch out of my rucksack and began to edge along carefully. After a few seconds I found the opening. The chicken wire had been cut through and left hanging. On the other side of it was a minute gap between some sections of plywood fencing that hadn't been joined together properly.

I held the wire back and went bottom first through the netting. Then I slid between the two bits of fencing. Directly in front of me was the side wall of one of the empty houses. I edged along it to the corner, then I peeped round and looked at the site itself.

The area that I could see beyond the houses was about the size of a football pitch. It was partially lit by the street lamps on the other side of the fence. Beyond that I couldn't focus on anything. Around me I could see a number of giant trucks parked at funny angles and some small works vans. A cement mixer was in the middle. I thought, for a moment, that it might have been the very same one that Eddie had died in but then I remembered that the firemen had had to cut that one apart to free his body. There was a line of giant piping that ran along the outside perimeter fence.

It seemed that this part of the new road site was mostly used for storage. The excavating and building hadn't started this far down yet. I looked over to the far corner and saw a couple of yellow helmets. I looked carefully round the area near me, what used to be the front gardens of the old houses. There were piles of rubble everywhere; the remains of the houses where people used to live.

Something moved over to my right. It made me jump and I swung round and was faced with a honey coloured cat sitting on what was left of a small brick wall. Its eyes were glittering in the light from the street lamps. I relaxed, watching as it lifted one of its paws and licked it lazily, keeping one eye on me as it cleaned itself. I huffed at myself for being so edgy.

I stood for a moment taking in the hush of the site, wondering if Nathan was there or not. Maybe he was, at that very minute, waiting on the corner of Lester Avenue wondering what had happened. The two yellow helmets had disappeared from view and

I took the chance to run round the side of the building to get into the middle house, the one that Nathan said the old man had lived in.

The number plate was still on the brickwork but the front door had long gone. Number 82. I walked quickly in and stood round the corner, taking care not to lean against the dusty walls, or to plunge into any cobwebs.

The darkness inside the house was thick and heavy. I took a few steps along the hall and felt my resolve disintegrate. I really needed my torch but I didn't dare turn it on in case anyone saw. I knew then that Nathan hadn't come ahead of me. It had been a bad idea to come. I turned around, meaning to go back out and leave the site.

I was fixing my rucksack over my shoulder when I heard the footsteps. I say heard but that's not really what happened. I *felt* footsteps. A very faint tremor in the floor made me stand stock still. A few seconds later there was another movement, a low creak as of a floorboard some distance away.

That was when I knew that someone was watching me.

I stood, glued to the spot and felt a pair of eyes on my back.

"Nathan?" I said. The word crept out weakly.

There was no answer but I was sure of a presence, a person standing in the shadows somewhere further up the hallway, their eyes wandering up and down my back, their movements slow and deliberate. I took a deep breath and walked briskly towards the front door and the light from the adjacent street. My shoulders were tense waiting for something, the sound of feet running, a touch, a rough pulling at my hair.

But nothing happened.

I stood outside and leant against the old door jamb. In the distance I could see three or four yellow helmets coming in the direction of the houses. As they got closer I could see the dogs pulling on their leads, surging ahead of the men.

Someone must have seen me. I turned back to the darkness in panic. I was going to be caught. The faces of my mum and my uncle jumped into my head. I was frozen with indecision. Should I go further into the house or face the security men?

I ducked into a door that was on my right. It must have been the old living room, or parlour, as my uncle sometimes called it. I slid commando-style along the wall to the cracked and broken windows and peeked out. The security men had stopped about twenty metres away. They were all shining powerful torches that sent beams of light into the darkness. If I just stood still for a few minutes they might go.

I flattened my back against the wall by the window and looked around the room that I was in. There was just empty blackness. I tried not to think about the noises I'd heard.

The voices came closer and I held my breath as the beams of light came into the room through the window frames. They swung from one corner to the other, like spotlights on a stage. I could hear one of the dogs barking and another whimpering. One of the men must have come right up to the window, centimetres away from me on the other side of the wall. His torch seemed to light up the whole room for a moment.

I followed the beam as it went across the far wall, swung up to the ceiling then down to the floor.

That's when I saw the body.

It was lying face down on the floor. I only had a glimpse of it, for a microsecond while it was illuminated and then it was submerged again by the darkness.

The shock held me to the wall, the blackness of the room closing around me, the silent form stretched out somewhere in the dark, less than a metre away from me. My voice was lost far down my throat and I closed my eyes, afraid to look in case I saw it again.

The voices from outside came closer but I couldn't move, could not speak to alert them. I heard them coming in the front of the house, the dogs' claws scrabbling on the wooden floor of the hallway. One man was coughing and another talking into a radio.

The light from one of their torches came through the door and settled on the head of the figure on the floor. The hair was long and I was reminded momentarily of Eddie Wolf's long hair as he lay in the drum of the cement mixer.

"My God, look here." I could hear the voice of the security guard outside.

I was still clamped to the wall, my mouth open, my voice in my boots somewhere as they came into the room. The three torches shone up and down the body and they were mumbling, "What's this? Not another one? Is it a tramp? My God, it's a young boy!"

I was behind them, hardly breathing, my eyes fastened on to the body as one of the men lifted the hair up gently and looked at the face.

It was Nathan Dyer.

"Oh, no," I said suddenly and the three of them turned round, aghast at finding me there.

"Oh, Nathan," I whispered. But he couldn't hear me.

12
Dead

Nathan Dyer was dead.

The police didn't actually confirm it until about three hours later, but I knew.

From the side his face looked rigid, his mouth slightly open as though in surprise or even shock. In the light from the torches I could see a lot of blood as well. Not red, the way you see it in films, but brown. A dark ketchup colour. After I stood there looking for a few seconds I turned away and felt myself retch deep in the back of my throat. I clamped the flat of my hand over my mouth.

One of the security guards grabbed my arms and his dog started to bark menacingly at me. "I've got her, I've got her," he said, as though I was the murderer.

I couldn't speak to defend myself. I couldn't even explain why I was there or point to the hallway of the house where I was sure I'd heard someone.

I was struck dumb with all sorts of wild thoughts whizzing through my head.

Nathan had got there early, had thought I hadn't turned up. He'd gone on, into the blackness of the old house. He'd only been there to try and help me. He stood for a few seconds in the hallway before an arm had grabbed him, a tap on the head, no wait, a harder, more deliberate blow, vicious even; he had collapsed... He'd only gone there for me, as a favour to me, because he'd liked me, just the way I'd liked him.

I think I started to cry sometime around then. I wasn't aware of it until I was jolted out of my thoughts by the sirens of the police cars. Then I tasted the salty tears at the sides of my mouth. They'd made my face wet and in the cold night my skin felt raw.

In the event I'd been right about the way he had died. Some time the next day Heather had rung me and told me about the pathologist's report. Nathan Dyer had suffered a savage blow to the back of his head with something like an iron bar. He wouldn't have known a thing, Heather had said.

It didn't make me feel any better.

I was at the police station for most of the night. My mum and my uncle came about one o'clock. She was upset, concerned for my safety. He was tight-lipped, giving me only a curt nod. A couple of times I tried to engage him in conversation but he turned away, his eyelids closing slowly. He was furious with me, I knew. It was our first case together and I had gone off on my own and got into trouble.

I allowed myself to dwell on it because it took my mind off Nathan Dyer.

I wrote out my own statement in the early hours. I put everything in. The items I'd found in the locker, the information from the girl with the tattoo, the registration number REM. The stuff Nathan had told me about the derelict house. I had several cups of tea and some sympathetic looks from the policemen and women who passed me by. Heather was nowhere to be seen. My uncle said that she'd been held up with another case.

A policeman came home with us to collect the stuff I'd found in Eddie Wolf's locker. The jewellery, the valentine card and poetry book, the money. When he left my uncle allowed his anger to come out.

"Patricia, you might look like a grown-up young woman but inside your head you're just a schoolgirl. You thrive on secrets and you think everything is a game."

"Tony, she's been through enough," my mum said, softly.

"No, no, she's not been through half enough!" He raised his voice. "I have my reputation to consider.

I'm asked to investigate a boy's murder and my niece sees it as a chance to play midnight hide and seek!"

"Tony, I've said that's enough." My mum's voice was a little harder.

"Couldn't you have phoned me? Let me know what was happening? Couldn't she have done that?" He was looking at my mum, a fake expression on his face as though he was really making an enquiry.

"I tried, you were out," I said, weakly.

"You be quiet!" my mum said, a sudden harsh note in her voice.

"Yes, you be quiet. At last a little agreement in the family about how to handle young Patricia."

"And you can shut up!" my mum shouted, her eyes glaring at my uncle. I held my breath. I hadn't seen her this angry in years. "I'm sick of this constant rowing between you two. I only asked you to give her a job because I thought it would be good for her and you. I thought you could get to know each other! Instead of that she's nearly been killed, she's been regularly put in a position of danger and all you ever do is tell her off and moan about her!"

"Honestly, I..." My uncle's voice had lowered. He had realized that he was on the losing end of an argument.

"You've done nothing but complain about her since she started to work for you."

"That's certainly not true..."

"Don't lie!" she snapped. My mum's finger was in the air, rigid, pointing into my uncle's cheekbone. "You can't wait to get shot of her. Well, here it is. I give you her resignation."

"Mum, I…" I stammered.

"I told you to be quiet!"

She started to walk slowly down the hallway, which forced my uncle to walk backwards.

"Don't be hasty, now," he said, turning towards the front door. "I know this kind of work can be stressful. A good night's sleep will do us all a lot of good."

With that he opened the door and went out into the street. I watched his back disappear down the pathway and towards his car. His shoulders seemed to be twitching with agitation.

Outside it was grey, the morning light settling lazily on to the houses and cars. In the distance I could hear the tinkle of milk bottles and the revving of a couple of early cars. A man ran by in jogging gear, a Walkman around his waist, plugs in his ears.

Everything was happening as normal. As though nothing untoward had happened in the middle of the night. As though Nathan wasn't just another name at the top of a police file.

I turned and without saying anything to my mum went up to bed.

I'd like to say that I hadn't slept, that I'd lain staring

at the wall trying to puzzle it all out. But after a few minutes of chewing at the sides of my fingernails, exhaustion tucked itself around me and I went off into a heavy sleep.

I didn't even dream about it.

I only remembered snatches, images of myself dressing up in my mum's clothes, something I'd done often as a small child. High heels as big as boats, their lethal stilettos scraping along the floor. Row upon row of glittering beads around my neck and heavy drop earrings making my ear lobes sore. Then another picture of myself riding a go-kart down a hill, my face a picture of delight, Billy watching from the side, a plastic spanner in his hand.

When I woke up the bright sunlight had forced itself between my curtains and was lying across my bed. The room was hot and I threw the duvet back off my legs.

The bedside clock said 11:26. I'd slept for six hours.

Nathan had been dead for more than twelve.

I lay there for a while listening to the sounds of the house. The Hoover was on downstairs and I could hear a thump from time to time as it bumped into chair legs and corners. When my mum turned it off I could hear the voice from the radio, a talk programme that my mum liked to listen to when she was at home. The bleep from the back door alarm sounded a couple of times. I imagined my mum taking out the vacuum bag to empty it in the bin.

Then the sound of the phone ringing, distantly from downstairs, as well as a low warbling sound from the extension in the bedroom next door. It stopped as my mum picked it up downstairs and I heard her talking in a low voice to someone on the other end of the line. There was a lilt to her voice that made me think it was Gerry.

Had he just found out about Nathan's death? What about all the kids at Second Chance? Did they know yet? What about Mr and Mrs Wolf? Had the police told them? Was it their business? Would Tony go to see them?

These were things I wouldn't find out because I was off the case.

I was glad. I didn't want to see the photos of Nathan's dead body as I had seen those of Eddie Wolf.

It was then that I remembered Eddie's gaunt, pale face, staring out of the mixer, photographed many hours after he had died. Nathan was only just dead when I found him. Not so frozen looking as Eddie. Maybe, if I had had the courage to touch him, he might still have been warm.

I felt a shiver that didn't materialize.

And yet they had looked similar, Eddie and Nathan; their hair, their faces, even their expressions. Nathan and Eddie could have been brothers.

Now they were both dead.

13
Teamwork

"You're just not a collaborative worker, Patsy," Heather said. She was sitting on the sofa in our living room, a china cup and saucer in her hand. My mum was just placing a plate of biscuits on the table.

"That's not fair," I said. It was over twenty-four hours since she had phoned me and told me about the cause of Nathan's death. Since that time I'd stayed indoors with my mum fussing over me. My uncle Tony had rung a couple of times. Billy had rung once but I hadn't returned his call.

"Thanks, Mrs Kelly," Heather said, taking a biscuit. "I shouldn't really, I'm watching my starch intake!"

My mum smiled but I could see she was ill at

ease. It was only the second time she had ever been with Heather and I could tell she didn't like her. Usually she would insist people called her by her first name but with Heather she'd left it at "Mrs Kelly". After a few minutes of straightening the cushions and fixing the leaves on a pot plant she went out of the room. I felt myself relaxing.

"Your mum's nice, Patsy," Heather said, looking thoughtful.

"What about the case?" I said. "What's happening?"

"The case? I thought you said on the phone the other day that you weren't interested."

"Well, no, not as an investigator. I just wondered whether there were any developments."

"Oh, Patsy!" Heather said. "If only you were more of a team player, what a good detective you'd make!"

Team player. It fitted in with the usual jargon that Heather came out with. It made everything sound like a gigantic game. Winners, losers, rules, prizes; maybe it was. I reached over and took a biscuit.

"Well," I said, "what's the latest score then?"

"The truth is, Patsy, the things you did, they opened up the case. I was sceptical, I'll admit. I didn't believe it was anything other than a bad accident. The things you found out about Eddie Wolf have thrown a completely different light on it."

In spite of myself I felt a tiny flicker of satisfaction at these comments. It was soon doused out though, by Heather's next words.

"If you had come to me with what you had we could have proceeded much more quickly. I had thought, after recommending you to the Wolfs, that there was a kind of unspoken agreement between us. Instead, you just went off on your own and now someone else is dead."

"It happened so quickly," I said, hardly hearing her words.

"You could have given me the information from the girl. It would have taken us only seconds to find out that the car belonged to the Director of SAFECO."

"But we found that out anyway."

"One of our officers saw him immediately and he told us that Eddie Wolf had been working for him as an informer, letting him know what the Fresh Air group were planning to do. At the moment I'm prepared to believe that that was all it was."

"Oh."

"And then the things from the locker. As soon as we got them the other night we were able to identify the jewellery as being part of a load stolen from a jeweller's in Hatton Garden some months ago."

"The Rolex and earrings were real?"

"Absolutely. Rubies, no less, worth, in total, about eight thousand pounds."

"Really?" I said.

"But if you had told us about these things earlier maybe you wouldn't have needed to go to the road site and maybe the boy would still be alive."

The boy. She was talking about Nathan.

"You think it was my fault?" I said, my voice louder.

"No, don't be so dramatic! I'm trying to say that if you had acted more with other people, even, God knows, that useless uncle of yours, then we might have seen developments in the case that could have prevented your friend being the second victim!"

"But when I did talk to you about it you weren't interested."

"I accept that. But with the information you found out it would have been different."

There was quiet for a moment and I could hear my mum rattling the dishes from the kitchen. *It would have been different*. It never had been in the past. Heather had always been sceptical of my theories. She had obviously forgotten that.

"I've had officers down at the site for the last couple of days. They've given it a thorough search, the houses, the rubble, the lot. There's no sign of anything hidden anywhere. I thought, initially, that we might find the rest of the jewellery haul there but no. If Eddie was looking for the stuff there then it's been removed."

"What about his girlfriend? Have you found her?"

"No, no one seems to know. I spoke to Cheryl Spenser, his probation officer, yesterday and she had no idea whether he was involved with someone or not."

"The girl with the tattoo?"

Heather shrugged. "Nowhere to be found. Maybe she's in the same place as George Exon."

I heard a knock on the front door and my mum's voice shouting, "I'll get it."

"We've got a small spot on a national TV programme tonight called *Crimefile*. We've got a rather hazy picture of George Exon that we'll broadcast. Maybe something will come up."

Heather stood up and straightened her skirt. She picked up her jacket off the back of the chair. The door opened and my mum peeped in; behind her was Gerry Lawrence.

"Someone to see you," my mum said, her face beaming.

"Pats! How are you?" Gerry walked into the room, nodding for a minisecond to Heather. His expression was serious, grave even. He put one of his arms around me.

"I'm fine," I said, gently disengaging myself. "How is..." I wanted to say *How is everyone at Second Chance* but I couldn't. It seemed hypocritical of me to care. I hardly knew any of them, really, or the people at Fresh Air.

"Everyone's fine," Gerry said, sitting on the arm

of the chair. He looked genuinely worried about me. I felt awkward at the show of concern. He took his small glasses off and started to clean them on the bottom of his T-shirt. It was the first time I'd ever seen him bother.

"I think I've met the full-time worker from Second Chance," Heather said. "Is it Beverley someone?" She was searching through her case for something.

"Bev Williams," Gerry said. He had his back to Heather and didn't bother to turn round when he spoke. I was embarrassed for her.

"That's right. Isn't she also a spokeswoman for Fresh Air? I think I saw her on the TV once."

"Yep!" Gerry said it proudly, replacing his glasses. His tone of voice implied that he wasn't going to say another word without his solicitor being present. Heather didn't seem to notice.

Beverley Williams, the full-time worker; I wondered if she knew about my breaking into the locker and taking Eddie's stuff.

"Anyway, Patsy." Heather clicked her case shut. "I have to go. I'll ring you later in the week, keep you in touch. Bye, Gerry."

"OK." I followed her out into the hallway.

"Don't forget, it'll be on telly tonight. Nine o'clock."

"Right."

"I'll let you get back to your friend."

I was about to open my mouth and explain that Gerry Lawrence certainly wasn't a friend of *mine*, but she'd opened the front door and was talking into a small portable radio. I watched her walk to her car, my hand up in a wave. She didn't turn round, though. She was so busy talking to someone she had forgotten about me.

The item on *Crimefile* couldn't have been longer than about three minutes. The presenter gave the background story and on to the screen flashed a picture of Eddie Wolf, the same picture that his parents had given me.

I was looking at it, enlarged to the size of the screen, when I heard raised voices from the kitchen. My mum and Gerry had been having some kind of row all evening off and on.

I turned the sound up. The presenter spoke briefly about the second death saying, "*In the course of investigations with a private detective, Nathan Dyer was brutally murdered, almost certainly by the same person who took Eddie Wolf's young life.*"

His picture was then shown on the screen; at least a picture of him taken when he was somewhat younger, his hair shorter and his cheeks fuller. It didn't look like him at all.

Finally George Exon's picture was shown. It was a side shot, part of a much larger picture taken by a reporter or police cameras when he was on a demonstration. Underneath was a phone number to ring.

Just then the door opened and Gerry came in.

"Have I missed this? I wanted to see it."

My mum followed him in.

"That's it! Walk away when I'm trying to talk to you."

"Not now, love!" Gerry said, his arms folded across his chest.

But my mum had turned round and walked out again. I heard her footsteps go up the stairs and a door slam overhead.

Gerry turned to me and shrugged his shoulders.

After Gerry had gone home and my mum had gone to bed I watched TV for a while. At least the set was on and there were pictures moving in front of my eyes. I was thinking about what Heather had said. If I had gone to her earlier would Nathan still be alive?

And then I started to think about Nathan and the kiss.

It was odd but in trying to remember it, the sound of his voice whispering in my ear, the feel of his mouth on my skin, I felt strangely unmoved. It was as if the memory of it had been erased. At the time I had been so thrilled, so exhilarated by the prospect of something with Nathan and now, only two days later, the feelings that it had aroused had evaporated. What was left was a kind of dull guilt that I couldn't really fathom.

The phone rang and stirred me from the settee. I clicked the TV off with the remote and went out into the hall.

"Hello," I said, looking at my watch. It was eleven-thirty.

"Patsy Kelly?"

"Speaking."

"My name's George Exon. I want to meet and talk to you."

"George Exon?" I said, adopting a loud whisper.

"The very same. I need to speak to you."

"Er ... I'm not actually on the case any more," I said, all sorts of warning bells going off in my head.

"I'm only speaking to you, not the police, not no one else."

"I don't know..." I said.

"And I won't even speak to you unless you promise me that you won't tell anyone. At least until long after we've met."

"Where did you get my number?"

"From Liz Wolf. Are you going to meet me or not?"

"I don't know..." Eddie's mum had given him my number. Even though I wasn't on the case any more.

"There's an all night café called Ricky's down by the docks. I'll be there between one and two o'clock.

Otherwise I'll be gone. It's up to you." The phone clicked and was dead. I stood looking at it.

Between one and two. Down at the docks. In the pitch dark.

I didn't know if I had the courage or the will to go.

I stood for a minute paralysed by indecision.

Then I rang Billy's number.

14
George Exon

Billy drove up in an old Ford. It was a car I hadn't seen before.

"New car?" I said. I was feeling awkward, wondering what we would say to each other.

"I got it at auction."

He was in his overalls and although his face was clean his hands were still grimy.

"You're still working on it? At this time?" I said. It was past midnight.

"I could say the same to you," he said smiling, looking at his watch. "You work on your case and I work on mine."

"Point taken," I said in a clipped voice and got into the car.

"To the docks, then," he said, catching my eye

with a wry smile and pulling away from the kerb.

We drove to a place about a hundred metres from the café. He was surprisingly friendly considering our recent row. I explained to him what had happened in the case so far, including the visit to the road site and Nathan's death. I stuttered a bit when talking specifically about Nathan, his name tripping guiltily off my tongue. Afterwards I wondered yet again what it was I felt guilty about. Being somehow unable to prevent his death? Or having romantic designs on him rather than Billy?

I didn't know. Fortunately, Billy was unaware of my feelings and just said the right things like, "You couldn't have foretold what was going to happen," and, "You did what you thought was right."

When I told him what Heather had said about me not being a team player and not going to her with the information I had he said, "Look at the times you went to her in the past! She wasn't exactly delighted to see you then!"

Which made me feel comfortably exonerated. Out of nowhere I had this rush of emotion and wanted to throw my arms around Billy and give him a hug. He had known what to say.

Don't get me wrong. I wasn't just looking for someone to take my side and even if I had been, Billy was the last person who would have done that. But it was nice to feel that I wasn't always completely in the wrong. In past cases it had been

Billy who had often been sceptical and wary of my theories. I had had real difficulty persuading him that my suspicions were warranted. Even then he had been all for going to the police, passing over our information to them.

But the police weren't always the best people. They were busy on hundreds of cases. Someone as important as Heather Warren dealt with one of my cases in five minutes. If the murderer didn't obviously jump off the page at her then she would flick through to the next file. Some of the police I had met in the previous months hadn't exactly filled me with confidence, indeed my own uncle had been a policeman for years.

But Billy saw the police differently. For him they were always the good guys who missed meal after meal and stayed up late at night to solve mysteries. They had neatly pressed suits and ties, or comfortable uniforms and solid hard hats. They were completely reliable, like the policeman your mum told you to find if you ever got lost as a young child. There was safety in the dark blue uniform whereas elsewhere there was only danger and chaos.

Even when Billy was eleven or twelve he was like that. If a kid was bullied in school he advised them to go to the police and bring charges of "assault". As well as that he was always telling kids to "sue" the teachers if they upset them. He had a real faith in justice.

We usually laughed him out of it. But when his parents had been killed the laughter had stopped because Billy *had* found some comfort in the uniforms, the talking radios, the sirens; the paraphernalia of the law.

I got out of the car to walk up to the café alone. The plan was that Billy would follow me a couple of minutes later, buy a tea and sit somewhere away from me and George Exon. After Nathan's murder I felt distinctly nervous about doing anything alone.

The café was hot and steamy and smelt heavily of grilled bacon. Even though it was the middle of the night it gave me pangs of hunger. I looked around. There were three or four tables full of older men, reading papers, playing cards, one or two turned towards the telly in the corner which was tuned into an American baseball game.

At the table furthest away from the counter was a young man. He didn't look like the man in the TV photograph but then that had been hazy. I took a chance and walked up to his table.

"Are you George?" I said.

He looked me up and down and said, "Sit down. You want a tea?"

"OK," I said, sliding along the seat.

He got up and walked across to the counter. He was small, slightly built, very young looking, his hair cropped like a skinhead. He didn't look anything like the other road protesters. When he brought the cups back I noticed the tattoos on his arms, floral with the words "mum and dad" woven into them.

I got straight to the point.

"The police are desperate to talk to you."

"I know. And I'm desperate not to talk to them."

"Why?"

"Be serious! First of all I break into the link road site intent on doing damage to the lorries and equipment. Then I run off when I think I hear someone and it turns out my mate is dead and the law is looking for me to help them with their enquiries. Am I likely to give myself up? No I am not."

"But they don't think you did it..." I started.

"That's what they say now. Just supposing I go along and give myself up. Do you think they're just going to pat me on the head and say, there Georgie, don't be a bad boy again? No they are not."

I bit my bottom lip. George Exon was having a conversation by himself. I saw, out of the corner of my eye, that Billy had come into the café and gone up to the counter. I could heard George talking about Nathan.

"And now Nath's dead. I, of course, am free and at liberty. How does that make me look? Do I have an alibi for that night? As it happens, I do not..."

I turned back to George and butted in, "George, I'm not the police. Presumably you wanted to see me because you had something to say."

"Yes," he said and looked down into his cup of tea. "You haven't told anyone you were meeting me?"

"I hardly had any time!" I lied.

"I've been in trouble with the police before, see. Not under this name though. That's how come they can't trace me. My name's not Exon see, it's false, like I was making a new start. And you needn't ask me what my real name is because I'm not saying."

"I wasn't going to," I said, with my hands in mid-air as though I was being held up by a gunslinger.

"Look, it was a funny business that night on the link site. Like it was last minute and only me and Eddie knew about it. There was a demonstration down the other end, see, so we thought we'd take advantage of the diversion. When we get in there Eddie says, you go on to the trucks, I've got something I want to look at and he walks off towards the old houses. So I stands around for a few minutes and then I went to look for him. That's when I heard someone. I whispered to Eddie to get out but I couldn't see him so I just legged it. I wasn't getting picked up again. I've been in a young offender's institution. Do you think I was going to go back there?"

He looked at me expectantly. I realized after a few seconds that he was waiting for an answer. I opened my mouth to speak but he said, "No I was not."

"So you didn't see anyone?" I said, a smidgen of disappointment in my voice.

"No. Except for Albie, there was no one around."

Albie. The name was familiar.

"As I was going back out through the fence, Albie was hanging around, just in the bushes a few yards down from the opening."

"Albie who?" I said. "Who is Albie?"

"Albie Forrest. The old guy who used to live in one of the houses." George looked at me oddly, as if I was stupid, as if I should have known who Albie was.

Then I remembered Nathan's story. *"Albert, Albie I think his name was ... he used to boast about keeping his valuables under the floor..."*

"But I thought Albie was dead," I said.

"Not when I saw him he wasn't," George said.

I didn't understand. "He was going in as you were going out?"

"I don't know, maybe. Thing is, Albie's always around that site. Up to a couple of months ago he used to kip in the empty houses every night. He was a lodger there, see. I think he got rehoused but he always kept drifting back there. We used to see him all the time. He was like a ghost; he would just pop up out of the dark. He made me jump once or twice. I thought the police would have picked him up by now. Then I see *my* picture on the telly. That's why I called you. Maybe Albie did see something."

"Is he still around, do you think? Where does he live?" I said, getting my pad out of my pocket.

"That's the problem see. He doesn't live any-where. I've only ever seen him hanging round the site at night, mostly down this end, near the High Road, where the old houses used to be. You'll easily recognize him if he is around. He's got a mass of white hair. He used to be a sailor, see," he added, as if that explained it.

I closed the pad. What had I hoped for? An address? An introduction card? A phone number?

George drank down the last of his tea. He was about to go. Thoughts were racing through my head. There were other things I needed to ask him.

"George, who was Eddie's girlfriend?"

"Girlfriend?" he said, a grin on his face.

"Was he involved with someone? It's important."

"Get serious. Eddie was just a kid. I know he hung around with Petra, from the protest group, but I didn't think he was involved with her. No, thing is, Eddie always had a fancy for older women. Now that I think of it, he was dead keen on his probation officer. He said she was lovely."

The door to the café opened and a voice boomed out, "Get the kettle on, Ricky," and a policeman walked in.

George Exon's mouth dropped and he looked at me with sudden fury.

"Stay calm!" I hissed. "He's not with me."

"He'd better not be," he said, standing up. He turned and walked to the door, keeping his distance from the policeman who had sat himself in a seat nearest to the TV and was talking to the man behind the counter. I caught Billy's eye as George swept out of the café. A couple of minutes later he got up and came over and sat down beside me.

"Did you get any information?" he said.

"Yes, and there's someone we've got to find."

15
Albie Forrest

It wasn't easy to find Albie Forrest. We left Ricky's café and went straight to the link site. We spent most of our time cruising up and down the empty road that was parallel to it. Three miles up, then three miles down. Some of the SAFECO security guards looked suspiciously at us as we passed back and forth, nudging each other and talking into two-way radios. There were one or two sections where the road moved away from the building works so we stopped the car and got out and walked towards the perimeter fence.

Driving along, the site area had looked deserted. Up close, though, it seemed there were small groups of homeless people everywhere; some sitting around roughly made fires, some huddled into doorways, some just sitting with their backs to the wooden fence, the words, PRIVATE NO TRESPASSING in bold capitals above them. They were mostly older people, say fifty or more, and some were clutching cans or bottles, looking resigned, with none of the swagger of some of the younger homeless that I'd seen.

We asked most of the people that we came across.

"Have you seen Albie Forrest?"

"Albie Forrest. Quite old, used to live in one of the old houses on the site."

"Albie Forrest, about sixty."

"Mr Forrest, white hair and beard, used to be a sailor."

Finally one old lady, in an ancient fur coat said, "Albie the sailor, my dear. I know him. He's usually around the Co-op."

We were close to a biggish set of gates that led on to the site and I was thanking the woman when Billy nudged me. I watched as the gates opened and a dark coloured Mercedes slid out. It stopped for a moment under a street light and a man got out of the driver's seat. He walked back a few paces to speak to a guard in a yellow helmet. Then he turned and walked back to the car. I could see the familiar letters on the numberplate, REM.

It was the same man that I had seen a couple of days before only this time he wasn't wearing a suit. He had sporty clothes on, joggers and a zip-up jacket, white trainers that seemed to glow in the night. Ronald Mitchell, the boss of SAFECO. He got back into the car without looking at us. After a few seconds of the wheels crunching over some debris from the site, the car sped away, up the empty road, and into the distance.

"That was my chauffeur, my dear," the woman in the fur coat said. "He's coming back for me later." And then she broke into peals of laughter. Billy and I looked at each other with consternation.

The Co-op was a giant supermarket about halfway along the new road. At least, it wasn't called the Co-op, that was a name that had hung on from the past. It was called CASHSAVVA. Billy drove there in no time. From a distance we could see the giant neon signs above the supermarket buildings, SAVE MORE WITH CASHSAVVA!

"Think he'll be up here?" Billy said, stifling a yawn. He was looking tired, his hair standing up at the front.

"I hope so," I said, "but if he's not then I think we go home and in the morning I'll go in and see Heather. That way she can't accuse me of keeping it to myself."

"What's this, a new leaf?" Billy said, pulling into the side of the road, close to the giant car park that skirted the store.

"Maybe," I said.

A new leaf. It didn't hurt to change, to take notice

of what other people said.

We walked across the road to a small group of people at the edge of an old outbuilding. There were some giant container lorries parked alongside so the area seemed cordoned off, self-contained. There were a number of dogs wandering about and one or two curled up beside a fire. I counted seven people sitting on sheets of cardboard, a range of covers over them and around their shoulders, a couple of men with their bottom halves zipped into sleeping bags. One or two of them sat up as we approached. As we got to them their expressions changed, from anticipation to disappointment. They'd obviously been expecting someone else.

After asking questions and receiving no replies, at least no polite replies, we realized what it was they'd been waiting for.

A small van pulled up about twenty metres away. A big man got out of the driver's seat and a woman from the other side. They were dressed up warmly in zip-up jackets. The man looked about my uncle's age and the woman a bit younger. The people who had been huddled around the fire began to move, to climb out of their covers and walk or shuffle sleepily towards the van. The woman opened the back doors and shouted, "Come on, Terry, I've got your favourite here!"

"Hold your horses, Doreen," a gruff voice said. A man who looked about sixty walked towards the van. He was followed by a couple of women who were linking arms.

"It's a charity soup delivery," Billy whispered.

Other people, previously curled up, came forward, some rubbing their hands together with the cold.

"Vegetable soup and some bread," the woman said.

"No croûtons, Doreen?" a voice said, followed by some laughter.

"Now, George," the woman's voice rang out.

I stood aside, embarrassed by what was going on. I'd had dealings with homeless people before and it had left me feeling dismal and helpless. Billy had walked across to the van and was talking to the man. I followed him but found myself standing a few metres away from the huddle of people that was collecting there.

"How's it going, Ray?" Billy said.

"Good," Ray said, carefully ladling some soup into a white polystyrene cup.

"I didn't know you did this," Billy said.

"Yes," Ray said. "Once or twice a week."

"Ray works down at the exhaust place at Bakers Green," Billy shouted over to me. He moved to the side to let a frail old lady pass him. "This is my friend Patsy," he said to Ray.

"Hi, what are you doing here, at this time of night? You're not courting, are you?"

Courting. It was an old-fashioned word but both me and Billy knew what it meant and we shook our heads furiously, avoiding looking at each other. Billy continued talking to Ray and I found myself looking away across the huge empty car park beyond the container lorries. *Courting.* It was something me and Billy had played around with for years, although nothing had really ever come of it. Just then Nathan's face came into my head and I remembered his words, *between you and me*, his mouth close to my skin when he said it, his breath hot on my face.

There was a bubbling of voices behind me as the previously sullen, unpleasant group began to sound like people at a social gathering; garrulous chatter and squeals of laughter. I looked round to see that Billy was joining in talking to one of the older women.

I closed my eyes to try and resurrect the picture of Nathan but it was gone. I felt this swooning feeling of regret. It was only momentary, though. I wondered what it was I was sad about, the loss of Nathan? Or the loss of the way I might have felt about him?

Across the car park I became aware of a single figure walking towards the group. He was about a hundred metres away and seemed to have come from round by the recycling containers. As he got closer to me I could see that his hair and his beard were white. They shone out under the street lights and made me think of Father Christmas. An amiable old man, a cheery smile, a generous nature.

As he levelled with me I opened my mouth to speak but he had a stern expression and seemed to be mumbling to himself. Eventually I said, "Mr Forrest," as if I were addressing a headmaster or a bank manager.

"Push off," he said.

Instead of speaking again I lost confidence and closed my mouth while he passed. He seemed to be mumbling to himself and hitting at something on his arm. My heart sank as I realized how difficult it was going to be to talk to him. It was all very well finding him, like the proverbial needle, but it was little good if we couldn't find a way to get him to speak to us.

I turned round to Billy and saw that he was still deep in conversation with one of the women. In his hand he had a polystyrene cup. After a couple of seconds he glanced up at me and I pointed frantically to the old man who had by this time got to the van and was waiting in line for his soup.

Billy came over to me.

"He won't talk," I said, with finality.

"He will," Billy said, with confidence.

"I'm telling you. I just know he won't!" Frustration was making my voice squeaky and so I stopped talking and banged my fists on each other until they started to hurt.

I watched as Billy walked up to him. He stood still for a second and then whispered something in his ear. The old man shrugged and Billy leant over and whispered again. The old man pointed to the soup container and Billy pointed towards his car. The old man nodded his head and continued queuing. Billy beckoned to me to go back towards the car.

"See you, Ray," I heard him shout as I walked across. I wasn't sure what was happening. Was Albie Forrest going to talk to us? How had Billy got him to agree to it? I let my fists unclench and hang loosely by my side. It was a relief. What had Billy said to him?

It wasn't long until I found out. The old white haired man walked across, his soup in his hand and his roll in the other. With his spare finger he was pushing away the strands of yellowing hair around his mouth. When he got to us he said, "I want the money first. Then I'll listen to what you have to say."

"OK," Billy said, raising his eyebrows at me. He put his hand in his pocket and got out a twenty pound note which he handed over.

So much for Father Christmas.

"You do remember the night I'm talking about, Albie, don't you? The night the boy was killed on the link site."

"Um." He continued drinking his soup, blowing

gently at the steam that was coming off it, then sipping carefully at the hot liquid.

"The dead boy was found in a cement mixer. It was Easter Sunday night. A Sunday." I was talking slowly, unsure whether he could hear me. I was even beginning to doubt whether he understood me or not.

"See, Albie, you were going into the link site when our friend was coming out. That's why we wondered if you'd seen anything." I was talking in the kind of tone you use for small children.

"I'm not stupid you know, sweetheart," he suddenly said, a nasty tone to his voice.

I sat back, surprised.

"I might look an idiot but I'm not. The only reason I'm here, see, is because I used to live in one of them houses. When they bought it up I was out on the street."

"Surely not," Billy said. "It's the law that all the tenants were rehoused."

"That's if you have a rent book, see. Me and the landlord. We had an arrangement."

"Oh."

"So now I live in the community, so to speak."

"But do you remember Easter Sunday?" I said, pulling him back to the subject.

"Of course I do. I'm not senile."

"No." But he was touchy. I pursed my lips and looked at Billy. He was looking thoughtful, as though he was still pondering the question of Albie Forrest's rights as a tenant.

"OK Albie," I said, with more bravado than I felt, "what did you see? After you went in the site. After you passed the boy on the tube embankment?"

"What makes you think I saw anything?"

"Because as you were going in a boy was murdered. You'd have to have been sleepwalking not to have noticed. And anyway, if you'd seen nothing I don't think you'd have taken my friend's money."

I was talking quickly, throwing everything in that I could think of.

"You're right there," he said. "I don't con people." His voice had lost its edge and he began to drink the cooled soup in great gulps.

"So what did you see?"

"I saw the lad on the tube line. I've seen him before and all the others. Long hair, earrings. They look like girls! No road here! No road here! They made me laugh. As if they were the first people who ever cared about anything…"

"After you passed the boy, you went into the site. What did you see?"

"I saw someone," he said, tantalizingly.

"Who?" I was getting exasperated.

I looked at Billy with annoyance. It snapped him out of his thoughts and he said, "This is a waste of time, Patsy. He knows nothing. He didn't see a thing."

"I did."

"It was probably going on a few feet away from him and he didn't see a thing."

"I bloody did."

"Maybe he just thought he saw something," I added, moving away from the car, as if I was getting ready to go.

"I saw the boy being dragged away from the house. The dead boy. I saw him being dragged down towards the cement mixer."

I stopped in my tracks.

"Who did you see? Who was dragging him?"

"I only saw him from the back. He had a jacket and a hood on. I didn't see his face."

I could have cried. After all this Albie had only seen the *back* of the killer.

"He had a jacket on. A dark jacket."

A dark jacket. That narrowed it down to about a third of the population.

"But it had some writing on it. French writing, across the back. Like handwriting, not printed."

"Embroidered?" Billy said.

"No, just fancy French writing. I know, see. Being a merchant sailor I know other languages. I can't speak much of them but I know what they look like."

"But didn't this person turn round?" I said.

"I didn't wait," Albie said. "I knew there was something wrong. I've been in fights and dangerous situations before in my life. There's a smell in the air. I knew something bad was happening."

I walked away and heard Billy talking slowly to Albie. After a few minutes he shuffled off and Billy and I got into the car.

"Will that help?" Billy said.

"I don't know. I'll take it to Heather first thing. It's up to her what she does about it."

"I'll take you home," he said and we pulled away from the soup van, the fire, and the cold people. I suddenly felt very tired. It was the second night's sleep I'd lost in only a matter of days.

We were about to turn back on to the main road and head home when we saw, parked at an angle, the Mercedes, its hazard lights blinking slowly in the night.

In front of it was Ronald Mitchell talking to two of his security men, their yellow helmets standing out in the dark. Somebody must have made a joke because they started laughing uproariously, Ronald Mitchell clapping one of the men on his back with glee. The three of them watched us as we passed.

Ronald Mitchell; twice in one night. He *was* a busy man.

16
The Jacket

I fully intended to go to Heather. There was never any question in my mind about that. I got home at five o'clock intending to have a couple of hours sleep but I found my mum in the kitchen, her head in her hands, crying.

"Didn't you get my note?" I said. My heart was sinking, thinking she had woken up and found me gone and jumped to the wrong conclusion.

She nodded her head without speaking.

"What's wrong?" I said, sitting down beside her.

She raised her head. Her face was pink and her mouth was in a grimace, her skin wet with tears.

"There's something wrong with Gerry. Something in the last week or so. It's not been the same."

"What do you mean?"

"He's just been sort of preoccupied. He seems miles away when I speak to him. He's late and vague about where he's going. This week it's been worse than ever. I've hardly seen him. What with you nearly being killed with that poor boy."

"Oh, Mum, I wasn't nearly killed."

"He's not as keen. I know he's going off me."

"Don't be silly, he adores you! Anyone can see that."

She was fiddling with the ring he'd given her, swivelling it around her finger. The giant orange stone was glinting under the kitchen light.

"I know you don't think much of him," she started to say.

"That's not true," I lied.

"But since me and your dad split, there's not really been anyone who makes me feel quite like he does. He makes me laugh, that's so important!"

"I know." I was rubbing her arm up and down.

"He cares about me. I know he's been married before and I know other women find him attractive…"

She stopped to blow her nose and I tried to think of something to say. Did other women find Gerry attractive? His protruding stomach and messy hair?

"He makes me feel … he makes me feel young! It's a cliché, I know, but suddenly I don't care about the wrinkles around my eyes and the fact that the skin on my arms is slack…"

"Mum, it's not!" I couldn't see her arms but I was sure she was wrong. "You've got no wrinkles around your eyes."

Of course at that moment, she did. Her eyelids were swollen and the whites of her eyes looked bloodshot. I didn't know what to say. I hadn't seen her in such a state for years.

"But that's the point. When he's around I don't care if I have or not!"

She was inconsolable. I made her go upstairs to her bed and lie down. I got some cotton wool from her dressing table and wet it with lukewarm water. I patted it over her eyes and forehead. After a while she seemed to relax and I pulled the duvet up over her.

I looked at my watch. It was ten to six. There was no time for me to have a sleep so I got into the shower and let the water drill through me for about ten minutes. I pushed my mum and Gerry out of my mind.

I got dressed in some black jeans and a flowered shirt. I felt warm, comfortable. About seven, I rang Heather.

I had her home number but all I got was her answering machine. I didn't leave a message. I rang the station and was told that she was on duty from midday. Maybe I did have time for a sleep after all.

But then I remembered George Exon's comments

about Eddie Wolf having a thing about older women, particularly his probation officer, Cheryl Spenser. Would it do any harm, I wondered, if I went to see her?

I remembered then that my uncle had already spoken to her. I made a grab for the phone intending to ring him right then and there to ask him what she had said.

Something stopped me though. I remembered his angry face and the hurtful things he'd said. I imagined him being exasperated with me for meeting George Exon.

I tapped my index finger a few times on the receiver. Then I went and had some breakfast.

Cheryl Spenser's office was in a building that backed off the old town hall. I went up to the reception area on the first floor and was told by a man in a uniform that Ms Spenser would be able to see me, briefly, in about five minutes. His name was Justin, at least that's what it said on his badge. When I was called in he said, "Good morning," in a sincere voice.

I don't know what I'd really expected a probation officer's office to be like. I had imagined somewhere rather cold, angular, sparsely furnished. In my imagination I had seen the actual person, the probation officer, rather like a stern schoolteacher, a head of year, someone who took care of discipline problems. I'd known that Cheryl Spenser was young, Tony had said that, but I had thought of her as being dark, thin, with pale bloodless skin. It was a silly image and was shattered as soon as I went into her office.

"Patsy Kelly?" Cheryl Spenser said, holding her hand out to meet me. "Do come in and have a seat. Can I get you some coffee?"

She was taller than me and had a powerful hand-shake. Her hair was corn coloured and cut straight around her jaw. She was pretty in the conventional sense, pale skin and deep blue eyes. She wore hardly any make-up and had a chocolate-brown suit jacket and skirt on and a yellow blouse.

At first I thought she looked quite young but when she sat back down at her desk she put a pair of heavy glasses on and she seemed to age instantly. Not just look older but more serious, more important. I fingered my own glasses and wondered whether new frames might do something for my image. Then I looked down at my black jeans and DMs and wished I'd put something a bit more grown-up on. I took my beret off and played with it in my lap.

The office was a surprise, too. It was brightly decorated with a small desk at the far end. Where I was sitting there was a small sofa and an easy chair at right angles. In between was a coffee table with a vase of flowers. There were posters all over the walls and the windows had bright blinds instead of the bars I had half expected to see.

"You want to know a bit about Eddie Wolf, when he was my client. I did have a long conversation with your colleague Mr Hamer, only a few days ago I believe."

She sat on the soft chair only a half a metre or so away from me.

"Yes," I said, intimidated by her brisk tone. I began to fold up my beret into quarters. "Some new information has come to light though."

"Really?" she said, glancing for just a minisecond at her watch. "How can I help?"

I took a deep breath and told her about the things I had found in Eddie's locker, the valentine card and the poetry book. I was watching her closely to see if she faltered at all as I described the items. It was disconcerting, though. All the time I felt that it was she who was watching *me*.

She said nothing, just "ummed", so I told her about what George Exon had said about Eddie having a crush on her. She smiled as soon as I said it.

"That's not unusual, I'm afraid. A number of clients form attachments to their probation officers. They see them as saviours of a sort."

"So did you ever notice anything?"

"Not what you'd call unusual, I can't say I did. I'm sure you don't always notice your admirers, Ms

Kelly." She looked me straight in the face.

"No," I said, not really as an answer to her question. She took it as such though and took her glasses off, which I took to be a sign that the interview was over.

"Was George Exon a client of yours as well?" I said stabbing in the dark, looking for a connection.

"Why do you ask?" she said testily.

"Because, the truth is, Ms Spenser," I said, fed up with her attitude, "I'm looking for some kind of lead here. There are two dead boys and I'm trying to find a way to explain their deaths. I would have thought you'd have wanted that too."

She looked at me for a minute, then she sat back in the chair and let out a long sigh.

"I have to be very careful," she said. "What my clients say to me is confidential. I cannot divulge anything."

"I don't want you to. I just want to know whether George Exon was a client of yours."

"No, he wasn't," she said, "although, and I expect you'll find this out anyway, Nathan Dyer was."

"Nathan was on probation?"

"Yes, about nine months ago. He was with me for three months. I believe that's how he and Eddie got to know each other."

"What for? What had he done?"

"I'm sorry, that's confidential," she said and

stood up. It really was time for the interview to end.

As I passed the man on reception I said, "See you, Justin," but he didn't reply.

Opening my own front door I could hear Gerry's laughter coming from the kitchen. That was a relief, he and my mum were friends again. I popped my head into the room and said hello.

My mum was sitting across the table from Gerry. She'd washed her hair and her face looked calm. She had a sort of secret smile on her lips as if only she knew the punch-line to a joke. Gerry was holding her hands across the table. Beside them was a vase of freesias that hadn't been there that morning.

"Hi, Pats," Gerry said.

"OK, Gerry?" I said, for once genuinely glad to see him.

I went upstairs and got my notebooks out. All the time I kept thinking about Nathan having been on probation. What had he done? I couldn't answer it but Heather would be able to. I got a fresh piece of paper and wrote down all the things I'd learned since the previous evening. As it got closer to mid-day I got ready to leave. I took a quick look in the mirror and saw myself. Cheryl Spenser's face came into my head. Her cool yellow hair and doll-like blue eyes.

I wasn't happy with the way I looked.

It wasn't the right time to be thinking of such

superficial things but I felt momentarily depressed and fed up with myself. I opened the wardrobe and rummaged around. I found a dark pink chiffon scarf and wound it round my neck a few times. I also pulled out a crocheted hat that my mum had bought me from a charity shop some time before. I pushed all my hair back and pulled the hat on. I found a waistcoat that I'd bought once and hardly ever worn and put it on.

In the mirror I looked different. Whether it was better or not I couldn't say.

I picked up my notebooks. They felt heavy in my hand. Nathan and Eddie Wolf were dead and I was worrying about my appearance. I shoved it all into my rucksack. I opened the front door and was faced with dark clouds. Some people already had their umbrellas up even though it didn't actually seem to be raining yet. I opened the cupboard under the stairs to get my mac out.

That's when I found the jacket.

My mac was underneath a number of coats and I wearily picked them off the hooks until it came out. One by one I replaced the army of jackets that were billeted there, resolving for the umpteenth time to clear the cupboard out.

I came across a dark blue jacket that I'd not seen before. I hung it on an empty hook and before placing another over the top of it I saw the writing on the back, RIVE GAUCHE. I stopped for a minute as the words washed over me, then I looked again. RIVE GAUCHE.

I stood for a moment, half laughing. *A dark jacket with French writing on the back.*

I felt inside the pockets and found some bus tickets and a packet of chewing gum. In the inside pocket there were some folded-up leaflets for the demonstration on Saturday and a small card that said NUS, Gerald Lawrence.

It was Gerry's jacket, there was no doubt about that. I hadn't actually seen him wearing it but it was his. On the back of it there was French writing.

I heard a laugh from the kitchen.

Then I remembered something that Nathan had said to me on the phone, the night he died. It had completely disappeared from my memory until then. *Gerry mentioned it tonight.* It was Gerry who had reminded Nathan of the story about Albie's buried treasure. That was why Nathan had rung me and told me to meet him. Gerry Lawrence had sent Nathan to the site. He had known that Nathan was going to be there.

Maybe he had planned it.

I stood in the hall with my notebooks in my hand.

Was it Gerry Lawrence who had killed Eddie? Had he realized that Nathan was getting close to the truth? Had he prompted Nathan to go to the site and then killed him too?

A guffaw of laughter came from the kitchen. It

was deep and behind it was the high giggle of my mum's merriment.

I sat on the stairs, my rucksack a lead weight.

I couldn't go to Heather with this information. I simply could not.

17
Gerry Lawrence

I was soaking wet by the time I got to Billy's house. The chiffon scarf around my neck was like a wilting tissue. The crocheted hat on my head seemed to have shrunk and felt more like a helmet. I walked straight in as soon as Billy opened the door.

I wasn't exactly crying but I was close to it.

"Calm down, calm down!" I could hear Billy's voice. After a minute or so of me walking up and down the hallway, blurting out bits of information, he put his arms around my shoulder and made me stand still, holding me tight. In other circumstances it might have looked like an embrace. This time it was to slow me down, make me stop, get some sense out of me.

He also gave me a cup of tea to drink and sat

across the table while I tried to explain what I'd found. After I'd got it all out he said, "You've left your mum with Gerry now?"

"No, no. Gerry went off to college. She's not seeing him again today. He's working at Second Chance tonight and then he's going back to his own place."

"It couldn't be Gerry. Honestly Pat, look at him. I know you don't like him much but he's not a bad bloke."

"I know, I know but…"

"But why would he kill Eddie and Nathan? You're surely not thinking that he's some kind of serial killer."

"No, no, nothing like that."

"Then what? It's just a jacket. You'll probably find out, when you go to Heather Warren, that there are thousands of jackets just like that in this part of London. That's the sort of information the police will have at their fingertips, Pat."

I was quiet, sipping my tea, thinking about Gerry Lawrence.

"You *are* going to Heather. That is what you said last night. You are going to give her this information."

"How can I?" I said. "How can I report the love of my mum's life to the police for the murder of two young men?"

"But that's exactly what you won't be doing.

You'll be giving the police information so that they can eliminate Gerry from their enquiries!"

Billy was sounding like a policeman. Billy was being sensible. It wasn't what I wanted to hear.

"Say he's innocent. Say I go to the police and they arrest him, find he has alibis, that the jacket is a common one. Say that happens. How's Gerry going to feel about me? About my mum?"

I kept thinking about my mum's miserable face that morning, her insistence that something was wrong with the relationship. That's all she would need. For me to poke my nose into it.

"What else can you do?"

"I can go to him. *We* can go to him. In some public place. Tell him what we've found, see how he reacts."

"It's *we* all of a sudden, is it?" Billy's face took on an odd expression.

I looked straight at him. "Billy, this isn't a good time to talk about me and you."

"Me and you?" he said, a smile forming on his mouth. "There is still a 'me and you' then?"

"I need your help," I said, ignoring his remark. I found my eyes avoiding his. I felt a stirring of guilt in my chest. "I need your help," I said again.

Billy said nothing and I picked up an empty cup of tea and pretended to drink from it.

On the table between us was a piece of paper. At the

top was Gerry's name. We were trying to list all the things that pointed towards Gerry's involvement in the murders. There was the jacket and the fact that Nathan had said Gerry had told him the story of Albie Forrest's treasure.

"I remember the day that Heather gave me and Gerry a lift to college, she gave him a very strange look. I thought then that he may have triggered her memory. He could have a record."

"Look," Billy said, trying to be organized, "are we agreed that the jewellery from the Hatton Garden robbery is the cause of the deaths?"

"It must be, what else could it be?" I said, not really sure. I'd ruled out the deaths having any actual connection with the road campaign itself.

"OK, so you think that maybe Gerry and Eddie did the jeweller's shop robbery?"

"It could be. Eddie had a record, contacts. Gerry was always short of money."

"It's a weak link," Billy said.

"Yes, but say they had done the robbery, hidden the bulk of the jewellery in that derelict house somewhere."

"But Eddie kept some of it out."

"Yes," I said. Something jumped into my mind. "And what about my mum's ring? The one that Gerry gave her. I thought it was paste. It's a giant orange stone. What if it's real? Amber or something? Worth thousands of pounds?"

"So they both did the robbery and hid the loot. But Eddie crept in to get it without Gerry knowing."

"Except Gerry found out…"

"And went to the link site…"

"Caught Eddie trying to take the jewellery for himself."

"That's it!" I said.

"But why kill Nathan?" Billy said.

"Because Nathan was poking around. Gerry had tried to fob him off with this story about Albie Forrest's treasure. Perhaps he began to worry about Nathan actually finding anything out and telling me."

"Unless of course it was *you* he wanted to meet on that site. You were the person who was doing most of the digging. Maybe Nathan saw him there and put two and two together."

"I don't know," I said, my voice low, unsure. It was something I'd never considered. That the killer had been after me on that night, not Nathan at all. I felt as though a great hole had developed in my ribs and cold air was blowing through it.

"It's only a theory. It may well have been Nathan he was really after."

The story sat between us like a garment that didn't quite fit. It was baggy, a little loose where it should have been tight.

"But why leave valuables, thousands of pounds

worth of jewellery, in such an open place? For all that time?"

"But it wasn't open. It was buried somewhere in a house that nobody ever went into. Who would ever think of looking there?"

Billy shrugged his shoulders and I looked down into my empty cup. I half wished there were some tea leaves for me to look into.

"Will you come with me to speak to Gerry?" I said, after a while. The palms of my hands were flat on the table, my fingers splayed out. He was looking intently at them. Without saying a word he put one of his hands on top of mine.

In the past I'd have been elated. Instead there was a niggle of discomfort in my chest. I gave a half-hearted smile. I wanted to pull my hand away, to sit back, away from Billy, in my own space.

"Please come," I said, and left my hand where it was.

18
Secrets

I rang my mum to tell her I was going straight out that evening. I couldn't face going back and seeing her in case she started to talk to me about Gerry. She sounded cheerful on the phone, told me not to be too late.

About seven Billy and I set off for Second Chance. When we got there the place was half empty.

"So this is it," Billy said, looking around.

There was a handful of kids on the computers and three or four at the coffee bar. The hall looked deserted and parts of it were in shadow, where the lights hadn't even been turned on. I looked around and my eye was caught by the notice-board. It was covered with pictures of Nathan. Billy had seen it too.

For a moment I was rooted to the spot. Nathan's face looked out at me. It gave me a kind of curdling in my stomach. My view of Nathan was now coloured by his death. I no longer looked at him with any desire or infatuation, not even his pictures. He was a dead boy; not the boy that I had wanted so badly a few days before.

Underneath the photographs was a table with small vases of flowers and some pot plants. There were notes in some of them. *Nathan, we'll miss you, Justine and Rosie; To a good friend, we won't forget you, Ross, Jamie and Bobby; Nathan, you'll always be remembered, Bev, Gerry, Ronnie, Jane and Petra, Project Workers.*

The pictures were taken at the centre itself. In them Nathan was doing things with the young people from the project. He was smiling at a potter's wheel, several girls laughing around him, his pot collapsing over his hands. In another he was painting a mural on to the side wall of the building. He had white overalls on and his hair was tied back. Two boys were standing by him dressed the same, looking industrious. There were two or three of Nathan relaxing, a cup of coffee in his hand, a newspaper in front of him, in conversation with a young girl. In the middle of the display was a picture of Nathan and the rest of the staff at the centre. At the back were Beverley and a couple of older men that I hadn't seen before. In front were Nathan and Gerry and a young woman. In front of them, cross-legged on the floor, were three young girls, one of whom caught my eye. I looked closer.

"That's the girl from the Fresh Air meeting!" I said to Billy. "The one with the tattoo who told me about Eddie and the man from the security firm."

Before Billy could speak I heard a voice from behind.

"That's Petra Donaldson. She's a part-time worker here. Well, she used to be. We've seen very little of her lately."

I looked round and Beverley Williams was standing a few metres away. She had a pile of posters in her arms and was dressed in overalls. Her long hair was tied back in a scarf. She looked as though she was in the middle of a spring clean.

"Beverley," I said, feeling a bit overfamiliar.

"What can I do for you?" she said, rather stiffly. I remembered then that she had a right to be annoyed with me. I had secretly searched the lockers in the private staff room. I had found Eddie's stuff and taken it away without asking her permission.

"I came to see Gerry Lawrence," I said. "I understood he was working this evening."

"Not this evening." Beverley squatted down and put the posters on the floor. She took one and unrolled it. Then she held it up against the wall and used a stapler to fix it there. "Gerry doesn't work this evening, never has." The staples made sounds like a shotgun.

"Any idea where he might be?" I said. The poster was for the demonstration the next day. The words *DEFEND THE AIR! STOP THE KILLER ROADS!* stood out.

She pursed her lips and then said, "You could try the Mulberry; it's a pub…"

"Down by the docks," Billy put in.

"Yes, he's started to go down there, I think."

"Thanks," I said. We all stood there for a moment and then I realized Beverley was waiting for us to go. She wasn't going to leave us there on our own.

"Look," I said, trying to find some words to say, "I'm really sorry about Nathan."

"Yes, so am I," she said, "we all are." She looked at her watch and I felt Billy's hand on my arm.

"We ought to get going," he said.

We walked out of the building and into the street. Even though it was evening and there was a sharp breeze in the air it still seemed warmer out there than it had been inside.

I remembered the photograph of Petra. She had been a worker at the centre as well as a member of the Fresh Air group. So had Gerry, Nathan, Eddie and Beverley. What did it all mean?

The Mulberry was in the smart part of the docks where several restaurants and wine bars had opened. It didn't seem quite the place to find Gerry

Lawrence. I was sure he had never taken my mum there.

The inside of the pub was smoky and the music was loud. I coughed a few times while Billy went straight to the bar to get a drink. I looked around for Gerry.

At first I didn't notice him. My eyes flicked around the main bar and then through some arches into a second bar in the back of the pub. It was dark anyway, with only spotlights here and there and some floor lighting, like on an aeroplane. I found myself getting irritated at the thought of him not being there. It was important that we saw him that night. I had promised Billy I would go and see Heather first thing in the morning.

Then I saw the back of his jacket. The words RIVE GAUCHE caught my eye. He was standing at the bar at the far end of the pub, presumably buying some drinks. I looked over to catch Billy's eye but he had his back to me as well. I could have walked on, gone ahead, sat down and started to warm Gerry up.

My confidence had deserted me, though. Instead of striding ahead I found myself leaning against the wall, a wilting flower, not knowing exactly what I was going to say, how we were going to bring the subject up. *"By the way, Gerry, did you murder Eddie Wolf on Easter Sunday of this year, only your jacket was spotted…"*

I could see Billy paying for the drinks and made myself stand up straight. I took my drink and said, "He's in the back of the pub. I've just seen him at the bar. He's wearing *the* jacket."

"Right, what's the plan?" Billy said.

I shrugged my shoulders. We hadn't got that far.

"I'll tell you what," he said, "let's happen on him by chance. Fancy meeting you, that sort of thing. Then you can start to tell him about the investigation. Tell him about Albie Forrest. I'll keep looking at him, see if there's any reaction. In the end you can drop the bit in about the jacket. See what he says then."

A number of young men in suits had just come into the bar. They were noisy, pushing and jostling with each other. They made me feel uneasy. Or maybe I was just anxious about speaking to Gerry. Either way I ventured nervously ahead of Billy and in the direction of the other bar.

I kept thinking about my mum's face if she ever found out about my seeing Gerry without telling her. There'd be a scene. I wasn't sure what would be worse. If Gerry was involved in the murders, or if he wasn't and he told her that I had thought he was.

We had to edge around an older woman who was sitting on a stool up close to a one-armed bandit. As we passed, the rollers came to a stop, thudding loudly. A split second later the machine started to pump out money. The noise seemed to be happening right inside my head. The woman sat impassively as the pound coins clattered into the dish.

When we passed through the arches and into the small bar I couldn't see Gerry at all. A surge of disappointment went through me. I thought he had left by some back exit while I was cowering, undecided, in the other bar.

I turned round and looked along the bar at the people with their backs to us, their five pound notes waving in the air like tiny flags. He wasn't there. I felt Billy nudge me.

"He's on the seat, over in the corner." Billy's voice was hesitant. I looked over towards the corner which was even darker than the rest of the bar. I could only see a couple in an embrace, the woman's arm around the man's back, her fingers in his hair. I frowned, looking at Billy then back to the corner.

A tiny spotlight beam picked out the words on the back of the jacket, RIVE GAUCHE. The man turned round and I saw his face. It was Gerry Lawrence, kissing some other woman, someone who wasn't my mum.

A fist of indignation rose up in my throat. He saw me at last and his mouth dropped. He leant over and whispered something to the woman whose face was still in the dark. He stood up and walked towards me.

I had an urge to slap him. It was as if my mum was there beside me and I was feeling her rage, her shame.

"Pats," he said coming up beside me, "it's not what you think." His hand waved casually towards the woman emerging from the corner. "She's just a friend, that's all."

I looked away from him, my eyes glued to the woman whom Gerry had chosen to be unfaithful with. I felt Gerry's hand on my arm as I recognized her face, her neat haircut, her smart suit. She was smiling as well, that seemed to make it worse, as if she were *happy* with what she was doing.

It was Heather Warren.

She came towards me; Gerry was still talking I think, still mumbling excuses when she came straight over.

"Patsy," she said delightedly, "what do you think? I've become rather friendly with your pal Gerry. He's really nice, fun to be with."

I looked accusingly at Gerry, then back to Heather. She didn't *know* that he was my mum's boyfriend. She just thought he was a friend of mine.

"Heather," I said wearily, "there's a couple of things you ought to know." I took her by the arm and we went in the direction of the Ladies.

Gerry was still in the bar even after Heather had left. He was sitting on a seat looking disconsolate, his hand nursing an empty glass, a cigarette hanging from the corner of his mouth. Billy was beside him. They didn't appear to be talking.

Heather had been visibly shocked when I told her.

"I'm so sorry, Patsy. I'd never have gone out with him if I'd known. I'd thought he was a friend of yours. I hadn't realized... Isn't that just typical of men?"

She had swept out of the Ladies, passed Gerry without a word and left the bar.

When I walked towards him, he stood up, shamefaced.

"Now look, Pats," he said, "this was a one-off thing. There's absolutely no need for your mother to know anything about it."

He suddenly looked shorter. I thought of my mum's words, "*I know other women find him attractive.*" His hair was a mess and his glasses looked smeared and in need of a clean. He was pathetic.

Billy stood up and hissed into my ear, "I've had a lot of trouble keeping him here. If you don't ask him soon about the jacket he'll be gone, believe me."

I sat down. "Gerry, do you mind if I ask you something?"

"Anything, Pats," he said, leaning across the table to hear me.

"Did you like Eddie Wolf?"

"Eddie?" he said, his forehead creasing. "Yes, I liked him. He was a bit of a rascal but he was OK."

"Did you see him on the night he was killed?"

"No."

"You didn't go anywhere near the site?"

"No. Look, about your mum. It would upset her if..."

I cut across his words. "Do you know Albie Forrest?"

"He's the old boy who's always around the site. What's all this about...?"

"He said he saw you on the site when Eddie was killed. He said he saw you carrying Eddie Wolf down to the cement mixer."

Gerry looked at Billy then back at me. "Is this a joke?" he said.

"Hardly."

"Pats, look, your mum and me, we have an *open* relationship..."

"Gerry, Albie Forrest saw a man dragging Eddie Wolf's body down to the cement mixer. That man was wearing your jacket. I have to bring this information to the police but I'm giving you a chance to go there first. If it was you that killed Eddie then you have to go and give yourself up."

"I didn't kill Eddie." Gerry looked flabbergasted.

"Why was your jacket seen there...?"

"It's not my jacket. At least it is now but it wasn't then. It was given to me, a bit after it all happened."

I was suspicious. It felt like Gerry was trying to wriggle out of it. "Whose jacket was it?" I raised my voice.

"It was Nathan Dyer's jacket. He gave it to me to put into the students' union jumble sale. It was a bit grubby when I got it but I had it cleaned. It's a bit small I know…"

"It wasn't your jacket?"

"No."

"It was Nathan's jacket?" I said, disbelief in my voice.

"Nathan's," he said.

"What does this mean, Pat?" Billy's voice was firm, quiet. I could barely hear him above the din of the music and slot machine paying out again.

"It was Nathan's jacket," I repeated uselessly.

"So it was Nathan who was dragging Eddie Wolf's body across the site that night," he said.

"Nathan Dyer killed Eddie?" I said. In my head there was a loud voice that kept saying NO.

19
Jewellery

It was an odd, awkward meeting in Heather's office the next morning. My uncle Tony, Heather and me all sitting round her big desk. Billy had had a commitment to pick up a car so I was on my own describing what had happened over the past couple of days; the meeting with Georgie Exon, finding Albie Forrest, seeing Gerry Lawrence's jacket and deciding to follow him. I mentioned the visit to Cheryl Spenser and the fact that Nathan had also been a client of hers. I left out the fact that Heather had been there when I approached Gerry Lawrence. I ended up with the revelation that the jacket in fact belonged to Nathan Dyer.

I felt strangely detached when I came to that point. It was Nathan's jacket, therefore Nathan was the one who had put Eddie Wolf's body into the cement mixer. For a few days I had felt an intense attachment to this person. Now he was turning out to be someone I wouldn't have wanted to know at all.

My uncle Tony was quietly taking notes of all the things I'd said. He'd been a bit miffed when I'd first phoned him, mildly annoyed at my continuing the case. But he'd eased off when I'd told him the things I'd found out. He'd picked me up at home and been friendly, in a distant sort of way.

I hadn't yet told my mum anything. It was something I was pushing to the back of my mind.

"So Patsy," Heather said, briskly, avoiding my eyes, "you think this Gerry Lawrence is telling the truth about the jacket?"

"I do," I said, looking her straight in the eye; *this Gerry Lawrence*, as if he were someone she hadn't met, hadn't been kissing only twelve hours before.

"The jewellery you tied down to a theft in Hatton Garden some months ago, am I right?" My uncle Tony was using his pencil to tick things off on his bit of paper.

"Yes." Heather, for once, looked gratefully at him.

"Are we to assume then that Eddie Wolf and Nathan Dyer are both involved in this?"

"It's possible," I said.

"They were on probation together," Heather said.

167

"So they'd both had experience of crime. Is it possible," I said to Heather, "to find out exactly what it was that Nathan was convicted of?"

"Yes, I'm waiting for that information to come through. Look, let's assume that they became friendly while on probation with Cheryl Spenser. They planned the job together. What then?"

"They hid the stuff in the derelict house. They planned to leave it there until the heat was off," my uncle said.

"Or until the house was due to be knocked down and the road built over it."

"Yes," I said. I pictured the old Victorian houses, standing proudly amidst the wreckage of the road site. I remembered Ronald Mitchell, the boss of SAFECO, standing in front of them, in his smart grey suit, his yellow helmet not quite fitting him. On the night we'd been looking for Albie Forrest he'd been wearing his sports clothes, brilliant white trainers, no safety helmet then, even though he'd been busying himself around the site.

"But Eddie Wolf decided differently. He wanted his half of the jewellery sooner." Heather was biting the end of her pencil, taking it out of her mouth with two fingers as though it was a cigarette.

"Or the whole lot," Tony said. "Eddie had decided that he wanted the whole lot."

"So Nathan killed him."

"Yes."

We sat there silently. I was looking hard into my own head at the scenario we had thought up, trying to imagine Eddie with his hands full of precious stones, Nathan coming up behind him. In the back of my mind I kept on seeing Ronald Mitchell, the boss of the security firm that hadn't got the link road contract. Eddie had been seen getting out of his car, ten and twenty pound notes cascading from his hands.

Eventually my uncle Tony spoke.

"It leaves one question."

"Who killed Nathan?" Heather said.

"A third person. Someone else involved in the robberies." Tony was drawing a line on his notebook, as if he were about to add a lot of things up.

"The security man, Ronald Mitchell," I said, looking hard at Heather. "You said, didn't you, that he claimed the money he was giving Eddie Wolf was to do with the Fresh Air demonstrations. What if it wasn't? What if he was selling the stuff and was giving Eddie his cut?"

"Ronald Mitchell is a straight bloke, Patricia. I can't see…"

"But it's worth looking into, isn't it? Mightn't he have contacts in the security world? In Hatton Garden? Say he heard about this jewellery. All he needed was to get someone to do it for him. He hears about Eddie through his dad and then Eddie contacts Nathan Dyer," I said.

"He's a successful businessman, though," Heather said.

"He is now. But at the time of the robbery his company hadn't been awarded the link road contract."

"That's true. That's why it made sense, when he said he'd been paying Eddie to give him information," Heather said, looking thoughtful. She made some notes on a pad and we all sat there for a moment.

"I can't see it myself," Tony said, closing his book, shaking his head from side to side.

"But you'll look into it?" I said to Heather, ignoring him. I stood up. I wanted to get off. There were things I wanted to sort out. My mum was at home and I had to decide whether to tell her about Gerry or not.

"Yes, leave it with us. And thanks for coming down here," Heather said. I noticed that her hair was messy and her face looked pale, the lipstick and rouge no longer there.

"Let us know. Either Patricia or myself will be in the office on Monday," my uncle said, smiling at me. It seemed I had a job again.

He walked ahead, out of the door and Heather came up to me.

"You do believe that I didn't know Gerry was your mum's boyfriend, don't you?"

"Yes," I said, and I did.

She nodded mournfully. Whether she was sad about what had happened or unhappy because she wasn't going to see him again I didn't know.

"I'll ring you, if any developments happen," she said and I left.

On the way out we had to wade through dozens of uniformed police officers who were lining up to get into minibuses and coaches. They were getting ready for the road link demonstration. There was an air of excitement, laughter and chatter, as though they were going on an outing to the seaside.

I followed Tony through and got into his car.

"Demonstrations!" he said. "In my day you didn't have time to demonstrate. You were too busy looking for a job."

I said nothing. There was no point.

20
Love

My uncle drove me home. He had a smile on his face most of the way there.

"I feel a real sense of satisfaction when a case is resolved," he said. I noticed him straightening his eyebrows in the rear view mirror.

"It's not exactly resolved," I said grumpily.

"But the links are there," he said, "and we're very close to joining them up."

I imagined a long gold chain and open link. Somewhere else there was another chain with a link that fitted. They were lying tantalizingly apart, waiting for us to put them together. I let this thought occupy my mind for a while. It meant I didn't have to think about my mum and Gerry Lawrence.

When I got home my mum was just returning to

the house after a run. Between great breaths she mouthed the words *five miles* to me. She came inside the house and walked up and down the kitchen slowly with her hands on her hips, her chest heaving in and out. Her face was flushed and she had a self-satisfied smile from ear to ear.

"Five miles," she finally said, "five miles."

"Well done, Mum," I said.

"When are you going to start running again?"

"Soon," I lied. I had taken up running from time to time. It usually gave me a stitch that felt like a bullet from a magnum.

"Tea?" I said, wondering whether that was a good time to sit down and tell her about Gerry.

"A bit later, love. I think I'll just cool down a bit and then have a shower."

"Is Gerry coming round?" I asked, hoping that he wasn't.

"He's calling for me. We're going on the demonstration. Are you coming?"

"I'm not sure," I said. I would have to tell her before then.

While my mum was in the bathroom I went to my room and decided to tidy up my wardrobe. This is a displacement activity. It's a chore I tackle when there's something much more important to do. It's a way of putting off an unpleasant task. I could hear the shower running and my mum's voice as she hummed a tune. Was I right to tell her? I didn't know.

While I was laying my clothes in piles on the bed, jackets, skirts, blouses, I began to think about love. I remembered Eddie Wolf's valentine card and wondered momentarily if it had been Petra, the girl with the tattoo who had sent it to him.

I squatted down and pulled out my shoes and boots from the bottom of the wardrobe. I counted two pairs of DMs, two pairs of plimsolls, some flat brogues and a pair of black leather court shoes that my mum had bought for me when I'd started work at Tony's. I'd hardly worn them. I picked one up and ran my finger through the dust that had collected on it. I remembered trying them on and my mum complimenting me on the way they made me look like a *smart young lady*.

She was going to be so hurt when I told her. I suddenly felt light-headed and sat down on the bed, my clothes around me in heaps, my determination to tell the truth crumbling. Was it really up to me to do it?

When I was younger I'd always imagined love to be like an emotional river and at some point in your life you simply fell into it. Once there you were submerged in a wonderful feeling of well being. Outside it was cold and lonely.

But it didn't happen like that. People weren't either in or out of love, like members of a club or not. There were degrees of love. I wasn't in love with Billy but I had strong feelings for him. Sometimes these turned to desire and I wanted to hold and kiss him. I hadn't been in love with Nathan Dyer but I'd experienced a powerful longing for him, quite unlike anything I'd felt for anyone else. Yet, overnight it had vanished.

Was my mum a little bit in love with Gerry or a lot?

I could hear the phone ringing from downstairs and warbling from my mum's bedroom. I rushed in and picked up the receiver.

"It's me, Heather. I'm ringing because I've got some news for you." Heather sounded tentative, as though she had to justify being on the phone to me.

"What have you got?" I said it in a businesslike way, not much friendliness in my voice. From the bathroom I could hear the water being turned off and the shower curtain being pulled back.

"Good news and bad news. We were right about some things and not others." She was using the word *we* as though she had been part of my investigations. I let it go.

"Ronald Mitchell has confessed to the Hatton Garden robbery, at least to the planning of it. He took us to his lock-up garage where he kept his part of the raid, necklaces, watches, rings, you know the sort of thing. He says that some of the stuff had been hidden in the derelict house."

"What about Nathan?"

"I'm coming to that. Ronald Mitchell says, and I believe him, that he did the robbery with Eddie, no one else."

"Nathan wasn't involved?"

"No. He may not have even known about it. It doesn't appear that anyone else did."

"But then, what reason could Nathan have for killing Eddie Wolf? If it wasn't to do with money?"

"Exactly. And then there's the other question. If Nathan killed Eddie, who killed Nathan?"

"So we haven't got the answer."

"We've got some answers, Patsy. We've arrested Ronald Mitchell and we're working on the theory that Nathan killed Eddie. I'm having the path. lab go over Eddie's post mortem details and see if there are any links with Nathan, fibres or hair. I don't know. It's worth a try."

"I wonder why he did it?" I said, more to myself than Heather.

"I don't know. I found out about his conviction. It was for grievous bodily harm. Apparently he beat up a lad at a factory where he worked, packing bread, I think. The boy was left with a scar, nearly lost an eye. Nathan's a bit of a mysterious character. We tried to find out other things about him, but nobody knew him very well. He didn't seem to have any close friends. He hadn't seen his family in years. He was a loner. Unless of course he had a girlfriend..."

"No, he didn't," I said.

"Oh, did he tell you that?"

"No, but I just know that he didn't."

"Well. It was just a thought. It might have thrown some light on him as a person if we could have talked to someone who had been involved with him."

"But the investigation goes on," I said, aware that my mum had come into the room wrapped in a towel with another on her head.

"It does, I'll keep you in touch."

I put the phone down. My mum was towelling her hair dry. In a while she would use the hairdrier and style it. Then she would put perfume on, maybe a bit of make-up. She would get dressed up and then listen for Gerry's footsteps up the path so that they could both go off on the demonstration. I couldn't stay in and watch all that.

"I'm going over to Billy's," I said.

I took all my stuff with me to Billy's, my notes and the file of things that Heather had given me. On the way round there I popped into a pizza place and bought a deep pan special.

Billy was surprised to see me, still a bit wary. His kitchen table was covered with small bits of engine and he had the radio tuned to a music station.

"I've already eaten," he said when he looked at the pizza.

"You might fancy some," I said, shrugging my shoulders. Were things ever really going to relax between Billy and me? I moved some of the engine bits and put my files and the pizza down on the table.

"What did Heather say?" he said, sitting down. He looked tired, but then he had lost a night's sleep recently.

I told him the details. I tried to be positive about it, after all an arrest had been made, stolen property recovered. As soon as I'd finished, though, he summed the situation up.

"So Eddie's death is nothing to do with the road campaign, it never was. Also nothing to do with the Hatton Garden robbery. We're back to square one then. If Nathan killed Eddie we need to know why. That might lead to finding out who killed Nathan."

"Heather says Nathan was a real loner but he seemed friendly and nice when I met him," I said, tripping over my words a little. He'd seemed much *nicer* than that but it was something I didn't want to tell Billy.

"Let's have a look at the photo of Eddie Wolf."

I handed it to him.

"This doesn't look unlike the photo of Nathan Dyer that we saw at the Second Chance Project," Billy said, "same hair and general colouring. Nice big smile. You could almost take them for brothers."

"Well, they're not," I said.

"Nathan didn't have a girlfriend, did he?" Billy said and I felt, for a moment, as if I was being cross-examined.

"No, he didn't." I said it with certainty.

"Good-looking bloke like him," Billy continued. "If Eddie Wolf had someone sending valentines to him you'd think Nathan here, bigger, older, wouldn't have had any trouble finding a girlfriend."

I was seething with frustration. I wanted to say, *all right, all right, I fancied him like mad and he liked me too*. I wondered if it would hurt Billy's feelings. Would he be upset the way my mum would be if she found out about Gerry Lawrence and Heather? Why did I feel that I'd let Billy down just because I had wanted someone else?

Betrayal. It was a bad blow, if you cared deeply for someone.

"You see, what I'm thinking here, Pat, is that Eddie was involved in some way with a mysterious woman."

"Yes." I was glad he was back to Eddie.

"What if Nathan was involved, too. Say with the same woman?"

"Nathan wasn't involved with anyone." I raised my voice.

"Why are you so sure? If, say, Nathan had a girlfriend who got involved with Eddie Wolf, that would be a motive for killing him."

"Nathan didn't have a girlfriend!" I repeated the

words slowly. Could Nathan have had a girlfriend? I hadn't let the thought bother me at the time. I'd been so sure that he'd been interested in *me*.

"Let's say he had a girlfriend," Billy continued relentlessly, moving a few screwdrivers out of the way on the table. The pizza sat in its box untouched. *Let's say he had a girlfriend. Why not? What did it matter to me?*

"Didn't you say that you saw Nathan talking to that girl with the tattoo, Petra, at the Fresh Air meeting? And she was the one who saw Eddie getting out of the Mercedes. Could it not be that they both were involved with her?"

In spite of myself I thought back to the day at the meeting. The first time I had seen her talking to Nathan I had wondered about their relationship. Petra. I hadn't known her name then but I remembered she'd been nervous and jumpy, desperate that no one should see her. At the time I wasn't sure who she was afraid of, there in the college. Could it have been Nathan?

"But whatever you say, it still doesn't answer the question who killed Nathan."

"No, but it goes part way. Imagine this. Nathan has a relationship, say with this Petra, and then Eddie comes to Second Chance and she's attracted to him. She and Eddie become lovers and Nathan is left out in the cold. Nathan, being an odd bloke, with a history of violence, does away with Eddie."

I kept a picture of Petra in my head as Billy was saying these things. She was small, slightly built, pretty but not stunning.

"Petra finds out that Nathan killed Eddie; maybe he told her, boasted to her. She knows he's going to meet you on the site and…"

"In a rage kills him," I finished the sentence. "Billy, Petra is a slightly built girl! How in heaven's name could she kill a big lad like Nathan? And why, why would she kill him? I'd have thought she would have *avoided* him. Or gone to the police."

"OK, not Petra then, someone else. Someone they both knew."

"Cheryl Spenser." The name came out of my mouth. I remembered her strong handshake, her tall frame, dressed elegantly in a suit and blouse.

"The probation officer?"

"Yes, for both of them. Nathan was on probation for three months. Maybe he had started an affair with her then. Or maybe he didn't have an affair but was just infatuated. She's a stunning-looking woman, very confident, sure of herself. For a while Nathan might have been the centre of her attention. Then his probation's finished and Eddie's is still going on. Could Nathan have been jealous?"

"Very possibly. Jealous enough to get rid of Eddie?"

"And Cheryl killed Nathan because…"

"You were getting close to Nathan. Maybe it

looked like the whole thing would come out. Exposure would have meant the end of Cheryl's career, everything."

"She's a tough woman," I said, thinking back to her assured manner.

"Did you speak to her?"

"I did, but…" I stopped. The story didn't quite fit. It implied that at some point Cheryl had let things get out of hand. It couldn't have happened like that. "She's very…" I couldn't think of the word to say, "very in control."

"Maybe she couldn't see any other way out of it. Maybe killing Nathan was her way of putting things back into her control."

"I suppose so," I said.

"We should go and talk to her, give her a chance to defend herself."

I looked at him for a minute. Did I really want to jump back into this again? I'd found out who had killed Eddie Wolf. Did I care who had killed Nathan? Hadn't he got what he deserved?

I opened the pizza box and took a slice. It was amazing. It was still hot after all that time.

21
The Woman

We found out Cheryl Spenser's home address from Elizabeth Wolf. When we got to her flat she was returning from a shopping trip, unloading Sainsbury's bags out of the back of her car. Her face wore no expression when she saw us.

"Cheryl, we need to have a talk. A serious one, about Nathan and Eddie Wolf."

"This is my day off," she said curtly. She was wearing jeans and trainers.

"I know that, but this is urgent."

"The least you can do is help me in with the bags." She motioned to the carrier bags and both Billy and I bent down and picked one up. As we walked up the stairs of the flats I marvelled at her dominance. Here she was, a murder suspect, and we were carrying her shopping bags.

Once in her flat she grudgingly offered us a cup of tea. We declined.

"I was going to ring you next week," she said.

"Why didn't you say that Nathan had been convicted of violent assault?"

"Because it was none of your business!" she said in the tone of voice that a schoolteacher might use. I felt put in my place. Billy didn't though, he was never one to be intimidated by schoolteachers.

"Surely it was relevant to the investigation. You of all people should know about co-operating with the police," he said, in his best complaining voice.

Cheryl Spenser took her glasses off and leant back against the kitchen worktops. Her grocery bags were lying on the floor, a couple of giant oranges rolling out of one of them. She turned, opened a cupboard and brought out a pack of cigarettes. She lit one and then inhaled.

"I only allow myself five a day now," she said, not really addressing her words to us. With no glasses and the cigarette in her hand she looked different again, no longer so cool and in charge but vulnerable, weary.

"You said you were going to get in touch. Have you got something to tell us?" I said.

"My first duty is to my client, not the police or the authorities, although some people would disagree with that. Every time some crime's committed that looks vaguely like something one of my clients has done the police come round. *Has Joe Bloggs been up to his old tricks again?* They can't believe, you see, they can't believe that these young people can change, that they can start to rebuild their lives."

I wondered where we were going with this. I tried to catch Billy's eye but he seemed to be concentrating on her words.

"So when the police come round asking about my talks and sessions with Eddie Wolf, of course I'm not going to give things away. My relationship with clients is confidential."

Billy looked at me for a minisecond and then looked back to Cheryl.

"Did you have a relationship with them, Cheryl, something more than professional?"

"No, no. Look, sometimes it does get close but not in the way you mean. Not romantic. They come to depend on us, on me, for all sorts of things. We become good friends. Sometimes they think, they hope, that it's more."

"Is that what happened with Eddie?"

"Sort of. But you just talk them through it. Help them to see that it's the situation they're in that makes them want someone to lean on. Once they're off probation they usually get on their own feet quickly enough."

"What about Nathan?"

"What do you mean?"

"Did Nathan become infatuated with you?"

"Goodness no. Nathan was quite a different young man to Eddie. Much more of a loner, much less easy to talk round. He was only with me for three months. I was sorry about that. I felt, when he left, that I hadn't really achieved much with him."

"How about Eddie?"

"I felt as though I had got somewhere with Eddie, but now, I don't know. You never really know whether you're getting through to them or not. He did get over his fascination for me, I'll tell you that. I got the impression he was pretty keen on someone."

"Who was it? Did Eddie tell you who he was involved with?" Billy said.

"No, but I did find something you might be interested in." She stubbed the cigarette out on the edge of a pot plant and walked across to her attaché case that was on a small table in the corner. After a minute she pulled out an envelope file. Eddie's name was neatly written on the corner of it. *EDWARD WOLF*. "I had a look through his file the other night after you left. I'm not totally opposed to helping the police," she added grumpily. "I make notes on the sessions we have so that I can remember things from week to week."

I looked at Billy, hopefully. Petra came back into my head. The mysterious girl who wanted to help me but was afraid of anyone seeing her. The girl who had worked at Second Chance and been a member of Fresh Air. The girl with the ring through her nose and the rose tattoo.

"Sometimes it's their birthdays," Cheryl continued, "or they're going out on special trips or a job interview. I usually make a note so that the next time we have a meeting I can ask them about it. I've got so many clients, you see, I would forget all the details of their lives."

I was holding my breath while she sorted through the file. Had Eddie told her the name of his girlfriend, the one who had sent him the valentine card? A first name, a nickname, anything?

"Here it is. I've made a note. I'll read it to you. *At last Eddie has an involvement with a girl. He is very pleased with himself. He says it's a secret for the moment because the girl is older than him and might be embarrassed for people to know. He says she's kind and pretty and,*' this is the part I thought might interest you, *'she has the longest hair he's ever seen.*'"

The longest hair. The longest hair.

Billy looked at me and shrugged his shoulders. It meant nothing to him.

It did to me, though.

"Thanks, Cheryl," I said. "We've got to go."

22
Demonstration

The demonstration was in full swing by the time we got there. There must have been about a thousand people walking along, holding colourful banners that said, DOWN WITH THE ROADS and FRESH AIR FOR LIFE. There were groups of musicians at different points along the way, a rudimentary brass band up at the front who were playing jazzy stuff, as well as some tambourines adding a mildly religious flavour to the whole thing. Further back was a steel band as well as groups of singers who passed us, leaving snatches of their songs in our ears.

The police were there as well, dozens of dark blue uniforms lined up like a human fence on the outside of the march. A few feet away from them on the other side of the road were the builders, not stopping for a second, their diggers and the lorries trundling back and forth over the same bit of road, their giant wheels rolling over and flattening the ground in front of them. The workmen were either steadfastly ignoring the demonstration or were just sitting, cockily watching the marchers as they passed them by, making comments and jokes to other men in yellow hats.

We stood by the side of the road and let the march go by us. We were given several leaflets about pollution and disappearance of the countryside. I noticed Billy reading intently through one of them. I saw my mum pass, walking hand in hand with Gerry Lawrence. She waved madly, calling me to go and walk with them but I shook my head. Gerry looked sheepish, his eyes catching mine for a second and then turning back towards the front. We were looking for one person. The Project leader, Beverley Williams.

All the way from Cheryl Spenser's we'd been trying to piece together what had happened. Beverley Williams was an important person at Second Chance. Nathan had been involved there first, for months before Eddie. Nathan and Beverley had had a relationship but for some reason Beverley had wanted it kept quiet. For professional reasons, perhaps. It wouldn't do for her to become romantically involved with a client. But then Nathan had developed from that into a voluntary worker. Perhaps the affair had gone on, or even finished.

Eddie Wolf joined. A vulnerable boy, recently looked after by the efficient Cheryl Spenser. He'd come into contact with another strong woman and this time it wasn't just infatuation. He really did fall head over heels in love.

Nathan Dyer didn't like it.

We couldn't get any further than that. On the way to the march we'd stopped at a phonebox and left a message for Heather Warren. Whether she would get it in time to come to the demonstration we weren't sure.

A group of people walked past us in long flowing dresses carrying armfuls of flowers which they handed out to bemused citizens who were standing along the pavement with their shopping bags and their rolled-up newspapers. A number of dogs were walking with them, with garlands of flowers around their necks. One or two of them didn't look too happy about it but walked on nevertheless.

We saw Beverley Williams close to the end of the march. Out of work she had let her long hair hang loose and from the waist up she had the look of a mermaid. There were some people with her, one or two I recognized from Second Chance. She didn't appear to be talking to any of them though, she looked preoccupied. Her eyes flicked across and saw us. Her face was expressionless. We walked through some banners and some women with children, and joined her.

"Beverley," I said.

"It's all right," she said, holding her hand up. "I know why you're here. You want me to tell you about Eddie and Nathan."

"We know about you and Eddie," I said, "we're not sure about the rest." I was being honest. There was no point in lying.

"Poor Eddie," she said, "he didn't deserve what Nathan did to him."

"No," I said. I noticed she hadn't included Nathan in her sympathies.

"He wasn't a bad boy," she said. I said nothing about the Hatton Garden robbery. It was very likely that she didn't even know about it.

The march was slowing down and we'd almost come to a standstill. I stepped out to the side, almost barging into a WPC who gave me a cross look and said, "Back now, back now." A giant digger rolled by, less than a metre away from some of the marchers, throwing up a shower of small stones with its caterpillar tracks. I was reminded of an army tank on manoeuvres.

"We've reached the rallying point," one of the stewards called. "Speeches will be in about fifteen minutes. Please sign the petitions that are circulating."

The marchers filed off the road on to a piece of

waste ground that hadn't yet been claimed by the road builders. In the near distance I could see the three old houses that were still standing behind the fences of the link site. The house where Nathan had been killed, not far away from the spot where Eddie had also died.

Beverley Williams must have seen me looking because she suddenly said, "Eddie shouldn't have died, you know."

I could barely hear her words above the din of the demonstration. Now that we were standing still, the sound from all the different bands was colliding in the air; a kind of musical pile up.

Billy shouted, "Why don't we move away? Then we can talk."

Beverley nodded her head rapidly and walked ahead towards a space on the far end of the waste ground, away from the speaker's platform and the bands, away from the festive atmosphere and the excited chatter.

She leant against the fence. Above her head were the words STRICTLY NO ENTRY. TRESPASSERS WILL BE PROSECUTED. A couple of policemen were looking suspiciously at us, talking into their radios. I wondered if they thought we were going to take a giant leap over the fence. I looked around for Heather but I couldn't see her. She probably hadn't got our message.

"I knew Nathan Dyer from years ago," Beverley

said. "I was a youth worker at the school he went to. There, I bet you didn't know that!" She smiled in a kind of triumph. It was true. It was a link we hadn't seen. I said nothing.

"So when he came to Second Chance there was an immediate friendship. We got involved with each other. I had to stop it, though. I would have lost my job. A project leader involved with a client. It's like a schoolteacher falling for a student. Very bad. Very bad."

She went on, "Nathan took it badly but after a while he was OK. He thought that once he became a proper worker at the Project, then things would be different."

"Were they?"

"I suppose they were but the trouble was that I no longer wanted the affair. The truth was that Nathan had a very nasty side to him. Very vindictive. It wasn't pleasant and it put me off him."

"And then Eddie Wolf came."

"Poor Eddie, he fell head over heels. It was very embarrassing. He always waited until I was on my own, then he turned up. I was never involved with him, though. Not after Nathan. I'd learned my lesson."

"What about the valentine?" Billy asked.

"I didn't send it to him, Petra did. She liked him but he wasn't interested in her. He just assumed I'd sent it to him."

"The poetry book?" I said.

"It was a present. I should have known at the time that it was a silly thing to buy. I found it at a jumble sale," Beverley said. She was using her hands to plait her hair at the side. I watched her weaving the strands through each other.

"A few days before Eddie was killed he came to my office. It was after the Project had closed. He was upset, something was bothering him and I talked to him. We were sitting close but there was nothing more. Nathan came in and thought that we were up to something. He was furious. I had to order him to leave, to threaten him with dismissal before he would go."

It was a side of Nathan I had never seen. I could hardly imagine him acting that way.

"Then a couple of days later Eddie was dead. That's when Nathan came to me, desperately upset. He'd gone after Eddie, he'd said, to teach him a lesson. He'd had a fight with him, put him into the cement mixer just to frighten him. He'd meant to turn it on only for a couple of seconds but he said that once he'd started the machine he couldn't stop it. He'd panicked he said, and not been able to move the lever back to the off position for a number of minutes. By that time Eddie was dead."

It was a horrible picture. I wondered whether it was true. Had Nathan just meant to frighten Eddie? Some clapping broke my concentration and I could see a speaker on the platform, looking at some sheets of paper and holding tightly on to a megaphone.

"I believed him. For weeks afterwards I just saw it as an awful accident."

"So why did you kill Nathan?" Billy said.

"I believed it for weeks," she said, ignoring Billy's question. "Then you came round. Nathan told me that an investigator was on the case. He said he wasn't worried, that no one would know. You remember, that first day in the office when we met. You left in a hurry? Well, Nathan saw the locker, Eddie's locker had been opened. We hadn't known what was in there. We'd not been able to open it, you see. There might have been letters to me, any kind of evidence. We just didn't know. I told Nathan to give himself up, to go to the police. They had thought it was an accident after all, why would they disbelieve him when he confirmed that?"

Beverley Williams looked at me and then Billy.

"But he wouldn't."

"Why didn't you go to the police?" I said. Surely she hadn't decided to mete out justice herself?

"There was no time. At nine o'clock he rang me and told me he was going on to the link site with you. I asked him what he planned to do; I kept on at him. In the end he said, *maybe she'll get what Eddie got!*"

My hand rose and clasped Billy's arm. For a brief

moment I didn't quite understand. Nathan had planned to do the same thing to me that he had done to Eddie Wolf.

"I knew then that it had all been lies. That he had meant to kill Eddie. I thought, I was sure, that he was going to kill you."

Billy put his hand over mine and I found myself chewing my bottom lip.

"I rang him and told him to meet me on site at an earlier time than he had arranged to meet you. I'd said I would help him set things up, get things ready. I didn't know what I was talking about but I wanted him there, away from where he was meant to be meeting you. I had some vague plan that I was going to talk him out of it or raise the alarm and have the security guards arrest us. When he came he was adamant, he was unpleasant. He said he'd implicate me in Eddie's murder if I didn't go along with him. He'd brought a crowbar with him. At one point he just turned away from me while I was in the middle of saying something so I picked it up and hit him with it."

I disentangled myself from Billy's hold and felt the beginnings of a shiver. I remembered Nathan's body, face down on the floor of that dark room. His expression, at the time, had seemed one of shock. In my mind though it took on a look of spite.

Beverley's face was calm, her head leaning back on the wooden fence. In the distance I could see the revolving blue light of a police car. I wondered if it was Heather. Beverley saw it too and stood up, almost to attention, a hardened look appearing around her lips.

"I'm not ready for this," she said. "I know what I've done but I'm not ready to be put in prison."

Without another word she walked abruptly away from us. I was taken by surprise. I had no idea what to do.

She'd slipped into the crowd and Billy was ahead of me after her. I saw Heather at the other end of the rally. She was looking around the site and I waved to her, still following in the direction that Beverley had gone.

Up ahead I could see Billy and just in front of him the long hair, billowing out like a veil. There were dozens of people and I kept saying, *"Excuse me, if you don't mind, can I just get through."* I wasn't sure if Heather was following me or had even seen me, I just kept following Billy.

When she got to the edge of the road I saw her stop. Coming along was a giant dumper truck, its back full of earth and stones, a haze of dust hanging around it like a low cloud. Beverley looked back. Billy was only a metre or so away and I thought it would only be seconds before she was back with us again. A moment's panic was all that she had had. But she turned her head away again to the opposite side of the road and all I could see was her long hair, hanging heavily over her shoulders. *"Excuse me, excuse me,"* I kept saying, but instead of getting closer to her Billy and I seemed to be pushed back by a wave of people who had started to shuffle about in between the speeches.

She stole a look backwards again and I could see that the dumper truck was extremely close, moving slowly along the road, its driver leaning out of his window making some comment to the marchers.

Her eyes caught mine for a moment and then looked quickly behind me. An expression of shock took over and I turned to see what it was that had upset her. Heather was coming towards me and behind her three uniformed policemen were weaving their way through the crowds.

Beverley made a run for it. Across the road. In front of the dumper truck.

I opened my mouth to shout something but nothing came.

She must have tripped on something because she fell to the ground just seconds before the truck reached her. The driver hadn't noticed her, though. He hadn't known she was there. He hadn't seen her.

I didn't hear her scream because there was too much noise.

I didn't see the truck hit her because my hands were over my eyes.

They stayed like that for a long time.

23
Mother and Daughter

I was sitting across the table from my mum. She was drinking some tea. Mine was untouched in front of me.

"She wouldn't have known what hit her, Patsy. It was just one of those terrible accidents."

I nodded my head, although I didn't really believe it. I remembered Beverley's face when she looked back and saw the police following hard on her heels. She had made a decision to run. She had known the truck was coming. How could she have thought that the driver would see her and stop in time?

"Gerry says there's to be a memorial service for her next week and a silent vigil outside the link site every night until her funeral."

She was being viewed as a martyr. A young woman crushed under the wheels of the New Road as it raced about the country demolishing everything in its way.

"Gerry says that the demonstrations could become more violent as a result of this. The protesters see Beverley's death as murder."

Gerry says, Gerry says, Gerry says. I wondered what Gerry would say when he found the truth about the murders of Eddie and Nathan. I wondered what they all would say. Even the newspapers didn't know the full story yet.

ROADS CAMPAIGNER CRUSHED BY TRUCK

Driver suffering from shock, "I didn't see her trying to cross in front of me!"

Yesterday's demonstration against the new link road in East London has ended in tragedy. Twenty-six-year-old Beverley Williams, campaign spokes-person, fell in front of a dumper truck while agitating against the builders. The driver of the truck, fifty-two-year-old family man Reg Beresford has been severely traumatized by the event.

Beverley Williams was attempting to lead marchers across the road and invade the works site, sources say. The tragedy occurred after a friendly demonstration in which workers and campaigners were frequently seen sharing jokes. Local Police Chief, Peter Riley said, "There was a huge police presence precisely in order to avoid this kind of incident. If the demonstrators had kept within the agreed areas it would never have happened."

The organizers of the protest are mourning the loss of a friend. A spokesperson said, "Beverley was a committed activist. She saw the spread of the roads as a deadly threat. She paid a high price for her beliefs."

Floral tributes are mounting up on the site.

"Are you seeing Gerry this afternoon?" I said, pushing the newspapers away.

"Probably. We're going to lay some flowers. Do you want to come along?"

"No," I said wearily. It wasn't the right time to tell her about Gerry and Heather. I wondered whether it ever would be.

"Are you going out with Billy?" she said. She was looking into a small mirror, licking her finger and shaping her eyebrows.

"Yes, we're going for a walk."

"A walk! What Billy, out without his car!"

"Yes," I said. Billy and I were heading up to the forest. We wanted to get away from the noise and the smell of the town, the roads and the cars and the protests. He wanted to talk to me, he said.

I didn't mind. As long as it got my mind off the past week.

Three dead people; three wasted lives.